The Water Drinkers

and Other Sketches of Paris in the Romantic Era

by Henry Murger

Translated and adapted from the French by

Zack Rogow

Boston, MA

The Water Drinkers

and Other Sketches of Paris in the Romantic Era

- *Les Buveurs d'eau,* published in 1854
- *Scènes de la vie de jeunesse,* published in 1851
- *Propos de ville et propos de théâtre,* published in 1853

Black Widow Press is an imprint of Commonwealth Books, Inc., Boston, MA. Distributed to the trade by NBN (National Book Network) throughout North America, Canada, and the U.K. All Black Widow Press books are printed on acid-free paper, and glued into bindings. Black Widow Press and its logo are registered trademarks of Commonwealth Books, Inc.

Joseph S. Phillips and Susan J. Wood, Ph.D., Publishers
www.blackwidowpress.com

Cover art: Samuel F. B. Morse, *Gallery of the Louvre,* 1831–33, Oil on canvas, 73¾ x 108 in., used by permission of the Foundation for American Art, Daniel J. Terra Collection, 1992.51.
Cover design and book production: Kerrie Kemperman
Photo of Henri Murger by Nadar, 1857

ISBN-13: 979-8-9911391-3-7

This book has been composed in Didot and Baskerville typefaces. The paper used in this publication meets the minimum requirements of ANSI/NISO Z39.48–1992 (R 1997) (Permanence of Paper).

Printed in the United States of America

10 9 8 7 6 5 4 3 2 1

Table of Contents

Translator's Introduction

Henry Murger (1822–1861) was the first author to write extensively about the bohemians and artists who rebelled against the values of middle class society. Bohemians and bourgeois dominance were both relatively new in Murger's time, the era of Romanticism in the mid-nineteenth century. Murger's characters were the forerunners of the beatniks of the 1950s, the hippies of the 1960s and 70s, and the "woke" culture of the present day. His bohemians have much in common with more recent alternative movements: a rejection of materialism; and an uncompromising commitment to a life devoted to pure pursuits, in art, or in society as a whole. Murger's fiction resonates deeply with contemporary culture.

Murger is best known as the writer of the collection of stories that Giacomo Puccini used as the basis of his delicious opera *La Bohème,* later the source for Jonathan Larson's equally savory musical *Rent.* Murger first published his sketches of artists and bohemians in Paris newspapers. The French author's famous characters, Rodolphe, Mimi, Marcel, and Musette, became celebrated in France when Murger turned those sketches into a popular musical in 1849 with the help of a playwright. Murger's stories were then collected into a bestselling book in 1851, *Scenes of Bohemian Life (Scènes de la vie de bohème).*

Today, Murger is known almost exclusively for creating the source material for Puccini's opera, but Murger was prolific during his brief literary career. His complete works span twenty volumes, much of it about artists and rebels. Little of that work has been translated into English. In this book, I've brought together three of what I consider Murger's best untranslated works:

- The first section of *The Water Drinkers (Les Buveurs d'eau),* published in 1854

- The initial portion of his book *Scenes of Youth (Scènes de la vie de jeunesse),* published in 1851
- A satirical sketch about how a cold spell disrupted the lives of Paris lovers, from *Sketches of the City and the Theater (Propos de ville et propos de théâtre),* published in 1853

Murger was a paradox. Despite his interest in bohemia, he dressed in the latest styles and frequented fashionable Paris night spots. In many ways, he was the exact opposite of the avant-garde characters he made famous, and who made him famous. Murger also had unusual medical issues that Jerrold Seigel describes vividly in his book *Bohemian Paris: Culture, Politics, and the Boundaries of Bourgeois Life, 1830–1930*:

> Ill for many years with a strange disease called purpura, which gives the skin a macabre color and apparently hastened his death, he [Murger] was repeatedly in and out of the hospital. His ailments gave him uncontrollable facial tics and caused his eyes to water. He was bald from his twenties.

Murger died young, at the age of thirty-eight, but by then he had already achieved the renown as a writer he had pursued since his early twenties. His life as an artist has many parallels with the main character of *The Water Drinkers,* the painter Francis Bernier. Like Francis, Murger was drawn into the world of bohemia without truly being part of it, since he enjoyed the pleasures of Paris' chic neighborhoods as much as the life styles of rebel artists. Also like his protagonist, Murger benefited from a trend in the arts that brought him momentary success, but neither of them became great in their chosen fields.

Murger was briefly a member and the secretary of an actual secret society of artists and writers in Paris called the Water Drinkers. They took this name because they were so opposed to making money on their art that they could only afford to drink water and not wine. The fellow travelers and acquaintances of the real-life Water Drinkers included some of the most renowned artists of the mid-nineteenth century: the poet Charles Baudelaire, the painter Gustave Courbet, and the photographer Nadar. But the core members of that group are mostly unknown today, immortalized by Murger's portrait of them more than by the art they created.

One fascinating side of *The Water Drinkers* is Murger's keen understanding of the dynamics in the art world. Murger described, as only an insider could, the rivalries, jealousies, and cliques that artists can fall into. He also showed accurately how little those have to do with creating great painting, sculpture, and literature. His portrayal of the way some dealers manipulate artists is also insightful and witty.

It's ironic that Murger's most lasting contribution to the arts was to create the story and characters for *La Bohème,* one of the great tragic operas. Murger's strongest suit was not tragedy, but a different genre: satire. His gift for irony is at its peak in the story "The Funeral Supper." In this piece of short fiction, Murger takes on many of the sacred cows of mid-nineteenth century artists and intellectuals. During the Romantic movement, there was a cult of melancholy, spleen, and suicide, similar to the punk and goth movements of more recent years. In Murger's day, many artists celebrated figures in life and literature who committed suicide, including the English poet Thomas Chatterton, eternalized in Henry Wallis' heartbreaking Pre-Raphaelite painting *The Death of Chatterton.* Johann Wolfgang Goethe also contributed to this cult with his novel *The Sorrows of Young Werther.* Murger's response to this romanticization of suicide was to create a comic send-up of it through his fictional hero, Ulric de Rouvres.

Ulric contemplates ending his days at a young age when he concludes that Paris high society is built on lies and deceptions. To escape this phoniness, Ulric takes refuge with the proletariat, disguising himself as a worker, the way princes of old put on rags to cavort with the peasants. Ulric believes he will finally find honesty and brotherhood among the salt of the earth. He's mirroring the ideas of the socialist and communist movements that first arose in Murger's time. Those movements placed all their faith in the working class and its ability to create an ideal society. In Ulric's adventures among the workers, Murger also satirizes the Marxist canonization of the proletariat. That proved to be a far-sighted perception of Murger's, since the era of globalization has turned some of the working class into opponents of progressive ideas. What I admire in Murger's satire is that the owners are subject to the same treatment as the workers: Murger aims his satiric squint at rich and poor alike.

Murger again pokes fun of high society in his comic sketch "Heated Romance in a Cold Spell." This nonfiction piece describes how the unusually severe winter of 1852–53 in Paris changed the lives of married spouses and their lovers.

A note on the translation: This book is not a translation in the traditional way that fiction is usually translated, word-for-word, or at least sentence-by-sentence. Murger was born two centuries ago; he was a product of a time with different values, and a commercial writer who rapidly churned out volumes to earn his living. For those reasons, I felt it better served both the author and the reader to adapt Murger's texts, rather than translate them exactly as written. I've tried to follow the practice of translators of plays, rather than obey the usual rules for translations of literary fiction.

When a play from a previous century is translated for the stage, the translator adapts the text to bring out what makes it relevant and interesting to contemporaries, preserving all the best lines and qualities of the original. That's what I've attempted to do with Murger's fiction. I've simplified the author's ornate nineteenth-century diction when it sounds too florid for the modern ear. I've also cut passages that don't move the story forward. In the story "The Funeral Supper," I actually deleted about half the text, since it includes a hokey love story, too sentimental and stereotyped for the taste of contemporary readers, or at least for my taste. I realize that this method for translating fiction is somewhat of an experiment, but I hope it's a successful one.

Zack Rogow
Berkeley, California; 2025

The Water Drinkers

The first section of Les Buveurs d'eau, *published 1854*

I. The Debut

Francis Bernier chose the career of an artist, despite his family's adamant opposition. Because of Francis' obstinate pursuit of painting, he fell out with his parents, who were in any case in no position to finance his studies. He soon found himself face to face with *the wolf at the door:* otherwise known as poverty. Accustomed to a life of ease, pampered in his family by a tender-hearted mother who anticipated his needs and happily indulged his every whim, Francis couldn't help finding this change in his circumstances somewhat brutal, once he was left to his own devices. Nevertheless, vainglory, which, even more than the love of art, motivates the masses and is the true source of transitory callings, kept Francis moving forward each time he was about to turn back.

The circle of artists Francis lived among bragged to him about the advantages of this unstable life, claiming it was the only true independence. When Francis questioned the advantages of a freedom that threatened to make him homeless, and which was draining his resources day by day, his artist friends told him that this existence unbound by servitude was a source of infinite poetry, and the best atmosphere for the development of the imagination. This daily struggle for the necessities of life was presented to him as a test of his talent, like the immersion bath that tempers steel. Francis was told that, just as battles make a warrior, a life of deprivation makes an artist.

At first, this negative way of life scared Francis. Soon he learned to like it and gladly put up with the trials of his apprenticeship. He worked with the passionate ardor of those just starting out. As with love, art has its honeymoon. Initially the fatigue of work has the same impassioned charm as the first days of love. In this period of wild enthusiasm, the privations that Francis had to endure seemed sweet to him. He thought of them as sacrifices that would yield ample rewards in the future.

A renowned master artist welcomed Francis into his studio without charging him fees, and Francis worked there for two years. One day, after class, the teacher pulled him aside.

"My friend," the teacher said to him, "I know you don't have the money to pay for these lessons, but when you first came here, you seemed like a person of good will. That's why I invited you to join my studio. Now you've worked here for two years. Usually that's more than enough time for me to form an opinion about a student. I can tell you now, you'll never be an artist. You would be smart to give up your ambition of becoming a painter. You're still young. You could start a new career and succeed in it, if you bring to it all the courage you show here—but in vain. As of tomorrow, someone else is going to take your place in the studio."

This was a poorly chosen moment to break the news to Francis, who actually thought he was doing quite well. He reasoned that his teacher was reluctant to keep him on because he was not paying tuition. That revelation, which should have put a stop to his pursuits, instead of presenting an obstacle, only spurred him on. Sometimes an artist has to think in a way that enhances himself in his own eyes, and deny the doubts that plague him. To do this, an artist injects himself with a kind of excitement that only lasts a short time, but is still strong enough to produce a work where the fever that inspired it is visible. And that's what happened to Francis.

In very little time he finished two canvases that were quite different from his usual work. It was painting tormented beyond measure, awkward, uncouth, showy; but it was actually painting. Both his faults and his qualities were boldly on display in those works, which weren't excellent, or even good. But it was truly impossible to pass by them without stopping, because they caught your eye. Many people, even after they reflected on this first impression, still could not figure out the attraction. And yet they felt it.

From then on, Francis never doubted his calling. How could he, when he saw the fuss his friends made over him? In Paris, young people often form groups, united by ties of chance, pleasure, or sympathy. Some of those ties seem obvious, others more chimerical. These groups are easy to understand: isolation is a very bad counselor for the discouraged: it's a good feeling, after a full day's work, to press the hands of one's friends, to live for a few moments in a circle of like-minded spirits. In your hour of weakness, you draw fresh energy from that collective perseverance. In the evening, returning home alone, you feel less isolated; you view again the same work that depressed you earlier, and this time you see it with pleasure. You fall asleep in a great mood, remembering a friendly conversation that sprinkled good dreams onto your pillow. The next morning, you wake up feeling stronger, your thoughts more wholesome, your hand more skilled. That's the positive side of fraternizing with other artists. But for these connections to produce useful results, those individuals have to be of real value and of a serious mind, and their sympathy has to stem from a healthy honesty. Nothing could be more miserable or ridiculous than artists who make their work a sort of begging bowl to collect compliments; nothing could be more dangerous than people who lavish praise on them—it's like being generous with counterfeit money. Unfortunately, honesty is rare. The very people who know each other the best, and who should be able to speak candidly amongst themselves, seem to have a tacit understanding that even if they venture a few criticisms, they're careful to blunt them, probably in the hope that when the time comes, others will treat them with the same deference. Vanity is an illness that everyone catches; a few people die from it, but more people live with it.

So Francis' friends were not shy about trumpeting their enthusiasm for his work. As long as that success remained just among themselves, those young artists enjoyed this carefully contained glory. Within their own obscure circle, they derived a certain satisfaction in proclaiming the success of one of their own. Implied in that praise, though, was a kind of threat to anyone who gained a reputation with the public. *Oh, when so-and-so's painting is actually exhibited, we shall see;* or, *When so-and-so's book is finally published, then we'll see.* The painting is shown, the book is published, and more often than not, the artwork is not noticed, the volume is not read. But if the opposite happens, if the public loudly echoes the success first voiced in that intimate circle of friends, then a rapid about-face takes place, and the friends ostracize the one the crowd has chosen.

In the meantime, Francis' friends paved his path with hyperbole. When they should merely have said, "It's not bad," or, "It's good," they called his work "a marvel," or "a miracle." They liberally poured him the tainted wine of their praise.

Not long after that, by chance an art dealer heard people talking about Francis' paintings, and he came to see them. The dealer was popular among that strange clientele for whom artworks are a sort of interior decorating accessory, and who leave it to their decorator to choose their artworks and the books in their library. That art dealer, who was quite successful, thanks to his numerous relations, had a storefront with a very visible location in a fancy neighborhood. Just being showcased in his gallery was instant publicity. The dealer readily bought at a low price the rejected works that would never have been purchased by serious collectors, and then placed them in the boudoirs of the most fashionable homes. He liked to launch young artists whose supple and fertile mediocrity allowed them to work quickly and produce on demand.

This questionable artistic destination was in some ways like a pawnshop. On the days when their material needs were snapping at their heels, artists came to him to consign their works, and received a paltry advance. If that amount was not returned at the end of a certain time period, always quite short, their consignment then became the property of the dealer, which is how these arrangements almost always ended up.

What's more, that same dealer extended credit so artists could buy supplies and provisions which they paid for in art, and this way, every year the dealer ended up owning a high percentage of the works he exhibited before they were even taken off the easel. It was usury disguised as patronage. Even though all the dealer's traps were well known, he didn't want for artists who voluntarily took part in this scheme, and they even felt grateful to be part of it.

This dealer was making a nice little fortune for himself. Not only that, he had his priorities straight: he put on the airs of a patron of the arts, conducted his business in an expensive carriage, and never went out without that golden fishing net he cast to make advantageous deals. When he entered a studio, the paintings trembled on the walls, like furniture that can feel the approach of the bailiff come to repossess it.

"I'll take on your paintings," the dealer said to Francis. "It might be risky. You're an unknown, but you have a certain extravagant flair—so I'll take a chance on you. If you're bought, I'll believe that your paintings are good, and I will *give* you talent. Here are twenty-five gold louis. It's madness, but what can I say: call me a fool."

The dealer tucked the two paintings under his arm, took the promised amount out of his pocket, threw it on the table along with his address, and left Francis dazzled by the brilliance of twenty-five gold pieces. Poets, who are ordinarily the courtesans of lies, have repeated in every lyric form known to humankind that the sweetest music is the first words of the first woman you love. That is more fluff than truth. An artist, especially if he is poor and discouraged in his patient obscurity, may say to himself a hundred times while looking at his work: "You should be providing for my life, but are you even alive? Am I even capable of breathing life into a work of art? And if I can, have I been able to communicate that?" For an artist who has suffered doubts about his work, not to mention exhaustion, deprivation, and all the ills the body is subject to, for that oppressive tyrant known as the mind, the sweetest music is actually the first money he receives for his work. There are so many lovely promises in the intimate melody of those coins that fall for the first time into the hands that earned them, even if the amount is only enough to buy a few green ribbons for the muse of Hope!

Francis often stood outside the dealer's gallery just to see what effect his paintings had on the passersby. Their opinions varied depending on who made up the groups. If the critical ones had brought arrows with them, his paintings would have been reduced to shreds. With others, the paintings elicited enthusiastic support expressed in exaggerations that were occasionally well reasoned, but more often than not, just prompted by ignorance. Francis' name, inscribed inside a cartouche mounted on the frames, was mentioned with disdain by some, with interest by others, and with curiosity by most. To put his name for the first time in the mouth of one of those Paris *flâneurs* who seem to have the gift of ubiquity, is like yelling back at an echo, or telling a secret to a gossip.

Three days after his paintings went on display, Francis inhaled the first delicious whiffs of celebrity. When he gave his address at a shop in the neighborhood of the dealer's gallery so his purchase could be delivered to his home, the owner of the store raised his eyebrows when writing Francis' name and complimented him on his paintings, which he had seen in passing. The very next day, in a café, Francis witnessed a heated discussion about his work between two young men he guessed were his peers in the arts. And only a few days later, the dealer who had promised to "give" him talent kept his promise, and sent him a little newspaper devoted to art with an advertisement promoting his works. Francis ran to show his friends, shaking the printed sheet in his hand, proud as a soldier who has just captured a flag.

His joy found few echoes. Those who had been the quickest to praise him gave him half-hearted congratulations; then came the quibbles of the pedants, tight-lipped and stingy with their words, as if each syllable cost them as much as a pearl or a diamond; then the advice of friends with their fists in their pockets, not yet daring to bare their claws, and who, of their five fingers, offered but one; the yellow smiles of a mouth that seemed to be chewing an unripe lemon; all the dodges in gestures and words at the bottom of which the monster Envy twists, creeps, and wheezes, like a slithering, cowardly, and venomous reptile hiding in the undergrowth and readying its poison before striking.

Even though he had little experience in this domain, Francis could have figured out the reason for the change he witnessed in his friends. But he was afraid that if he followed their behavior back to its source he would discover a vile motive for their cooling off, so he preferred not to become too suspicious. He continued to spend time with them, in the same congenial manner as before. Two very different reasons prevented him from breaking off relations where, on one side at least, all honesty had disappeared.

Where would I go, Francis asked himself, *if not to their homes?* Habit, that invisible bond, adds every day a thread that makes it stronger, and against which willpower is a hundred times less powerful when it wants to escape from an emotional trap.

And to get to the bottom of it, if the warm feelings that tied him to some of his friends were weakened by their actions and comments, vanity, that voracious cancer that feeds on everything, found ample sustenance in all the envious remarks that he provoked among his friends—since envy is the sharper edge of praise. To envy someone is to wound them with an arrow dipped in a balm that brings pleasure.

Of Francis' unexpected treasure, one part was quickly consumed by debts he incurred during his days of hardship. Francis was young, he was raised with ideas that he had frequently heard described as miserly, but which he had still not abandoned. He didn't like accruing debts because the due dates preoccupied him; they robbed him of his peace of mind. Obliged to fall back on credit, he applied for it with humility, almost with shame. His uneasy integrity did not sit well with the promises he made out of immediate need, since he knew he could only get cash from a pawnbroker. The first time he signed a promissory note, he trembled as he wrote his signature, and two hours later he ran back to the lender to redeem his I.O.U., and return the objects he had purchased on credit.

"You acted like a fool," said one of his friends about this incident. "Every creditor is like Monsieur Dimanche in Molière's *Don Juan.* If you naively go and pay the merchants cash, they greet you without even taking off their hats. Debts are a necessity of life. They're what the bastards of luck inherit. You have creditors when you're young, just like you have mistresses, because you have to live, you have to love, but creditors don't prevent you from being an honorable man."

All these subtleties amused Francis, but they failed to convince him. He found it repugnant to resort to credit. Even simply asking for a loan from a friend who was temporarily in a position to help him, he still felt he had to describe in minute detail the reasons why he needed his support. One could easily find such scruples useless, tiring, even pretentious. There was pride in Francis' hesitations, that was quite possible, but there was certainly delicacy in that pride. Even if Francis' sentiments were not always understood by the lender, that doesn't mean they weren't real. Francis found true satisfaction in saving the receipts for the loans he had repaid, loans that his creditors did not even expect to be paid back. Once he was free of those, he felt more in charge of the little that he possessed, and he made use of his time in a freer manner. The heavy footsteps of debt, which resounded like a summons to work, no longer echoed in the stairwell. If nothing else, he could now allow himself the luxury of sometimes being lazy. He could go out and come home when he chose without dreading an ill-timed visit from a lender. When he went shopping or took a walk, he no longer had to alter his route in order to avoid *streets that were being paved,* a colorful expression which, in a certain parlance, meant locations where one owed money.

Still in possession of a few gold louis and now accustomed to sobriety, he could foresee a time when he would no longer have that small fortune at his disposal, and he did not know how he could live frugally enough. Abstinence begets excess. So many wishes he had formerly repressed, so many unsatisfied desires demanded his attention that he had to listen to them. Those desires are the creditors one usually pays first, and human nature prioritizes them. Also, each of those gold pieces seemed to have wings. No sooner had he put one in his pocket than it ended up in his hand, and then just as quickly, poof! It was gone. Artists don't store provisions like ants: when they get money, they're like sailors whose boat has just docked in port. If you speak to them about Tomorrow, they seem not to understand the word. That's because Tomorrow is a saint whose day does not appear on their carefree calendars.

Toward the end of this period in his finances, the young painter made a personal connection that little by little distanced him from his former circle of acquaintances, and that could have exerted an influence on his destiny as an artist much different from the previous events we have seen. The story of this connection is quite curious in many ways. The characters who figure in this tale represent little-known aspects of a certain life, the poverty and joys of which have rarely been described by a historian willing to tell the whole tale. For that reason, we begin with the story of Francis Bernier and his friend.

II. Man with the Glove

In the galleries of the Louvre Museum where he painted copies of the old masters, in classes at the School of Fine Arts, or while leafing through books in the library, Francis Bernier encountered several times a young man he exchanged small favors with, in the way that art students often do. This young man's physiognomy did not at first glance inspire confidence. He spoke very little, and he was one of those people who gave only abbreviated answers to discourage anyone from asking him more questions. He didn't turn away when approached in an amiable or neighborly way, but he also didn't seem eager for those conversations to lead to further exchanges.

A number of times Francis saw him in the company of some young men who appeared to be his friends. One day, he saw one of them bring the young man a little package that was well wrapped. His neighbor slipped it carefully under his rough smock, the type that fishermen wear; and right after that, he quickly left his easel and exited the room with his friend. This interruption was unusual for that young man, who never took a break from his work during the eight hours he devoted to copying paintings.

Francis, who had followed him with his eyes without thinking, was suddenly seized with the desire to find out what his neighbor was up to. He tailed the two of them at a distance, as far as the Gallery of Antiquities. Once there, the two young men separated. The one who had brought the package headed for the vestibule that led to the exit from the Louvre, and the one who had received the package went into the depths of the museum's ground floor. From a safe distance, Francis could see him in the far corner of an empty room. The young man, no doubt thinking he was well hidden when he sat behind a sculptural group, glanced around to make sure he was alone, and then took out from under his smock the object that had been brought to him, and he unwrapped it.

Francis could not get any closer without being heard or seen, and at that distance, he normally would not have been able to discover what the young man was up to, but the first gesture of the subject of this spy mission revealed right away the motive behind all his precautions. Francis blushed profusely and left the gallery to continue working at his easel, deeply affected by what he had just witnessed.

Five minutes later, his neighbor also resumed his work. Francis did not dare raise his eyes to look at him because he was afraid his facial expression would betray his act of curiosity, which had been so sadly satisfied. Once Francis' first blush of embarrassment had passed, he examined his neighbor, who was starting to work again with renewed ardor. Francis noticed a few breadcrumbs stuck to the young man's cravat and to the rough fabric of his smock.

These details told him nothing new, but what he had learned did tell him volumes more about the situation of that young man and his friends than any of Francis' suspicions had revealed. They all wore the sad uniform of poverty proudly endured. In their garments, ghosts of a former elegance, one could easily read the daily struggles of a hardworking needle, applied to clothing that was threadbare as the result of time, rather than neglect. One could guess that their sorry hats, shapeless and nondescript in color, had been touched by hands that knew how to bow. Among the poorest intelligentsia, there are revealing affinities that allow them to recognize one another right away, but an instinctive modesty prevents them from showing that they're members of the same unfortunate fraternity. They seem to fear they would wound one another by an admission that could be seen as a form of begging. It's only when they surprise each another in the flagrant delight of poverty that they drop this pretense. Those whose destiny has sheltered them from want are unaware of such nuances, and they have no idea how much pride an empty pocket can hold. That piece of bread smuggled with so many precautions and devoured in secret exposed a type of mysterious drama that the selfish majority refuse to believe exists.

Pity is not strong every day, and there are spectacles that make it slink away. Francis himself, who thought he had endured the most trying of times, realized that he had at least been spared the hardships that his neighbor was experiencing.

This young man's face, by a quirk of nature, bore a striking resemblance to the portrait painted by Titian known as *Man with the Glove.* If he had dressed in the same manner and you met him in the galleries of the Louvre, you would have taken him for the resurrection of the model who had posed for that masterpiece. He was no doubt aware of this coincidence, remarked on by all the regulars among the copyists, and his vanity was certainly flattered to hear strangers comment on this when they visited the galleries, because he almost always worked in the gallery of the Italian School, the location of the canvas for which he was the living twin, like the identical brother in Plautus' comedy of errors, *The Menaechmi.* That was how the young man got his nickname, the Man with the Glove. He was often gossiped about by the girls and young women who came to the Louvre to copy the work of the old masters under the watchful eye of a mother or a maid, though a few worked on their own.

When the Man with the Glove arrived, more than one curious head turned and followed him with looks that would have satisfied the vanity of even the most conceited, but he paid absolutely no attention to them. When, by chance, a woman was painting next to him, he avoided any incident that might have provided an excuse to strike up a conversation, and he would never have thought of offering to give up his spot if he had the best light.

The Man with the Glove, who intrigued Francis to the point of making him commit the previously described indiscretion, sparked his curiosity even more since the adventure involving the piece of bread. But this sort of curiosity, always reprehensible if aroused only for frivolous reasons, had become almost excusable because it was motivated by real interest. For several days, Francis studied his neighbor with great care, making every effort to wiggle past the Man with the Glove's usual reserve. But the young man was wary, and every time he saw Francis ready to cross the line that separated banal chatter from actual confidences, he quickly reverted to silence and a leery attitude that thwarted even clever attempts to open him up to questions.

One afternoon, one of the young man's friends came to pick him up, probably on an urgent matter, because the Man with the Glove gathered his belongings in haste, forgetting on the frame of his easel a letter he had taken out of his pocket and whose envelope he had made into a twist of paper, the kind of little stump that artists fashion to smear charcoal and shade their drawings. Francis waited until everyone working there had left at the hour when the galleries closed, and pretending that he had forgotten something, he got permission from the guard to return to his easel. Then he grabbed the letter and left the museum without anyone witnessing his indiscretion. It was reassuring to Francis that his conscience did not raise any alarms about this. He was obeying one of those stubborn impulses that hypnotizes a person, and that someone unquestioningly follows in order to attain a desired goal, and that Francis would have ignored under normal circumstances.

Once he got home, Francis opened the letter. One glance revealed that it would tell him what he had wanted to ask the Man with the Glove. The letter was dated some time ago, and the creases in the paper showed that it had already remained a considerable time in the pocket of its owner. Here's what the letter said:

Paris, 25 January 184…

My Dear Brother,

Please forgive us for not responding sooner to your last letter, the one you sent from Le Havre. A great misfortune has befallen us, but thank God, it didn't have all the terrible consequences we feared at first. One month ago, Grandma had a fall in one of the houses that she cleans. They brought her to our home with a broken arm. Imagine what a state we were in! When this unexpected setback occurred, there wasn't even one sou in the house. I realize that wasn't smart. Grandma didn't want to worry us—you know how brave she is—so she tried to convince us it was nothing. She didn't even want us to call a doctor, and she said she could heal herself with camphorated alcohol. She just asked us to light a candle for her at the abbey. Our friend Soleil went to light the candle, but I ran out to get the nearest doctor. That was actually Doctor ***, whose office is not far away.

We've been to his surgical practice two or three times. You remember how harsh he was, and the atrocious jokes he made when he was sharpening his instruments for an operation.

When I arrived at his office, he had just left his clinic and sat down to lunch. Ten people were already waiting to see him. The door was blocked and two of his lackeys were guarding it. Impossible to enter. I guessed it would be a two-hour wait. I could almost hear Grandma's cries. Imagine my anguish! I would gladly have gone to a different office, but Doctor *** is the best surgeon in Paris. Suddenly, a person I believe is his secretary, left the doctor's dining room, and through a crack in the door I saw that it was on the same level as the garden. Immediately I left the antechamber, telling the servant I'd be back. I had a plan. I had arrived at the office by crossing the courtyard of the house, so I had noticed there was another entrance from the garden. Once I saw that no one was looking, I slipped into the garden, walked halfway around, found the door to the dining room, quickly opened it, and then appeared right before the doctor, whom I found in front of roughly a dozen plates, with a servant standing next to him, a napkin draped over his arm.

The doctor looked as if he'd seen the devil, and he almost jumped out of his chair. His first bout of anger was directed at the servants: he wanted to fire the lot of them. He yelled; he swore so loudly that the plates trembled. The poor devil serving him turned whiter than the napkin he was holding. I remained very calm; I was determined not to leave without the doctor. His fury didn't scare me. I've had dealings with a professor at the School of Fine Arts who has the same disposition, and I knew how to handle those with natures prone to violent eruptions. Quickly I gave him the reason for my being there, I made excuses for my highly unusual entrance, and I concluded by asking him to make an immediate house call. While speaking to him, I tried not to act as if I believed he would raise any objection to my appeal, which I presented as an absolutely necessity. I could hear him roaring inside, and I could see in his eyes that he would just as soon have me hurled out the window; but since we were on the ground floor, a puerile act of that sort would have accomplished nothing. My boldness flustered him so much that to release some of his fury, he began slicing at the tablecloth with his knife.

"Monsieur," he finally said to me, "even if I had broken my own arm, I would not allow my lunch to be disturbed. I wake up at five in the morning, I work half the night. For twenty-five years I've devoted three quarters and a half of my time to science and humanity. Pleasures—I only know them by hearsay; and the world—only by piercing it with a lancet or with a scalpel in my hands. The least you could do is to leave me in peace while I eat my lunch. You can wait in my antechamber like everyone else—their needs are just as pressing as yours."

What the doctor said was true, but his little speech was pretentious, and something of a pose. He has not been spared the vanity of great men. He had the posture of a sculpted bust that only looks good in bronze, but luckily for us, and especially for Grandma, the doctor was actually made of flesh and bones.

"Monsieur," I responded, "the patients waiting for you don't need you as much as my grandmother. Their condition can't be that serious, since they managed to get here all on their own, while my grandmother needs you to go to her."

"I'll drop by your house later today," he said to me. "Leave me your address."

"Monsieur," I answered in the same confident tone, "my grandmother is in terrible pain. An hour's delay would mean a great deal of suffering for her. I promised her I would bring you with me."

"At least wait for me to finish my lunch."

I could see that even as we were speaking, he was already eating twice as fast. "Your meals take too long," I said, half joking, half insisting. "Ask for your dessert, and then let's go." I handed him his hat and his cane.

He was stupefied. "You're not going to keep me from having my coffee, are you?"

I was going to make that small concession, but I realized it would lead us in the wrong direction. With men like that, if you take one step back, you lose the advantage you've gained. He was in my grasp, and all I had to do was squeeze a little tighter. "We'll make you coffee at my house," I said. He could not hold in his amusement any longer, and he broke out in a laugh of Olympian proportions.

That great man, used to making everyone in the hospital tremble, laughed like a school boy who checks in every direction before sneaking out of his house.

"The patients waiting for me—bah! They can wait. I know them, they probably just have a few little booboos. Is it far?"

"Only a few steps," I said.

"Good thing!"

On the way, the doctor confessed to me that if I'd approached him by appealing to his compassion or by begging, he would not have abandoned his cutlet. "You found the crack in my armor," he said. And he continued as if he were talking to himself: "Ah, willpower—what a force! Apply it to day-to-day events, it's a powerful lever; apply it to science, and you're halfway to genius."

"And what if you apply willpower to art?" I asked him, just out of curiosity.

"I don't know," he answered brusquely. "Artists are their own creatures. Everything about the human system is upside down in them. Any deviation from the ordinary order of nature is a phenomenon, and every phenomenon is a monstrosity. Artistic talent is a cerebral disorder. Look at madmen! They're almost all poets."

"And poets?"

"They're all madmen. Poetry is a delirium that follows rules."

Even though I was preoccupied by other matters, I couldn't help feeling proud of being on familiar terms with a man who a quarter of an hour earlier had spoken about having me defenestrated.

When we arrived at our house, the doctor stopped suddenly and gave me a look that filled me with anxiety, and he said to me in a tone that was too serious to be sincere: "Are you aware of my standard fee for a house call?" He has, as you know, the reputation of looking out for his own interests. I was even more stunned that he seemed to be waiting for my answer before going further. "It's very expensive," he continued.

I could only keep on the way I'd started. "It doesn't matter to me how high your fees are," I said, "because I can't pay you anyway. Here we are, doctor." And I showed him the stairway. He glared at me again. Seeing the mask of calm conviction on my face, he put his hand on the banister and led the way upstairs, nimble as a cat.

On the fourth floor landing, he paused to catch his breath. "How many more steps?" he asked.

"Seventy."

"That makes a hundred and twenty," said the doctor. "Well, I've climbed more stairs before."

We resumed our ascent. Once we got to the top, he turned toward me: "You didn't tell me about the ladder. You can damn well bet your grandma is only going to require one visit."

That brutal manner, so wounding for a grandson and especially at the point when we could already hear Grandma moaning, did not make me alter my facial expression. I could guess what that man was like. His sharp eye cut through my soul like a scalpel, and he could feel the pounding of the anger I had to contain in order to bear his harsh words. One word, one gesture that would have betrayed the sadness I was concealing, and the doctor would have escaped the spell of that dominating willpower that had drawn him here, as he had confessed. Not a muscle trembled in my impassive mask. I could feel suppressed tears in my throat, falling like hot droplets. We entered the apartment; it was high time.

As soon as he set foot in our home, the doctor became another person. "My child," he whispered to me, "have a seat and cry long and hard. Break something—that'll soothe your nerves. You realize I was only joking, right? I'm pleased with what you did to get me here, and I think you'll be pleased with me. And now, introduce me to your grandmother." And then he took off his hat. I wanted to hug him around the neck, but I knew he didn't like displays of emotion. So you see, just as I'd guessed, it was the experience that he was after. Since he couldn't get paid for this house call, in order for it not to be a waste, he got his fee in the form of research. My brother, those men of learning, they, too, despite themselves, are raging egotists condemned by their tyrannical ideals to seek everywhere and forever.

The doctor approached Grandma. When she tried to stand up to greet him, he made her sit back down and spoke to her in such a sweet tone that I couldn't believe he was the same person.

Once he had examined the fracture, the doctor ran his glance over our home. He seemed to sum up for himself our situation when he saw the darkened fireplace, the walls that oozed yellow tears of dampness. We were in the middle of the worst and saddest days of winter. A December tempest beat its wings against our poorly fitted windows. Poverty, and everything that goes with it! said his eloquent grimace.

Then he spoke directly to Grandma: "My good woman, your condition is not serious." Grandma put her hands together as if to thank him for this good news. "But you will probably have to recuperate for a month or six weeks. I'll give you a note for the director of the hospital where I'm the head physician. They'll put you in the best room under my care, and your grandchildren will be allowed to visit you every day. If you have any complaints about the sisters who care for you, just let me know."

Hearing these words, Grandma turned completely pale and looked at us as if to say, *Are you going to make me go?*

"Grandma dear, don't worry, you're not going," I said, embracing her.

"What?" said the doctor, who didn't understand. He was astonished that his generous offer was greeted by silence and embarrassment all around.

"Monsieur," I answered, "Grandma doesn't want to leave us, and we don't want her to leave."

"No, not on your life, as long as my children are near me, I'll never go there," said Grandma. "I'd be all alone in the world, and at death's door. I would rather die in the street than cross the threshold of that hospital. Even the word 'hospital' makes me shudder."

"You're exaggerating!" said the doctor. "The recovery from these sorts of accidents takes a long time, and they're expensive to treat. My good woman, you're not being reasonable, nor are your grandchildren."

"I can't stop working for more than a week," said Grandma. "The Good lord knows that. I know he'll create a miracle so I can get back on my feet in a week's time."

At this point, Soleil returned. Grandma asked him, "Did you do what I told you, my boy?"

"Yes, Grandma," Soleil responded, "I lit the candle myself, and while it burned, I put in a word to your patron saint."

The doctor shrugged his shoulders and pulled me aside. "Help me persuade your grandmother," he said to me. "It's madness for her to stay here. Look around you!"

"We'll sell everything to take care of her," I said, in response to his plan.

"I hope you throw in the walls." He was referring to the sad state of our dwelling.

"The only thing I agree to do is to convince my grandmother that she won't be confined here for long," I said. "Even the idea of not working for a long time is more dangerous to her than her wound. As far as the care and all she needs to treat her condition, Grandma has five or six grandchildren who will do everything they can for her. When destiny brings a great misfortune like this, Providence brings us resources we didn't foresee."

"So, you also believe in those little candles?" grumbled the doctor.

"Not so loud," I said. "When someone suffers but still has a spark of hope, whether it's from belief or superstition, don't blow out that meagre light that can save them from the horrors in the shadows. In a case like this, impiety is pointless."

"What?" the doctor said, changing the subject, "you mean there are five or six brothers here, and amongst the lot of you, you can't manage without your grandmother working?"

"Grandma only has two grandchildren, and my brother isn't here now. The others are actually friends we call brothers, and they're as loving and grateful to her as we are."

With that, the doctor gave in. "I'll come back every day," he said to me. He walked up to Grandma and spoke to her in that tone that some doctors have that could convince a corpse that it's still alive. He gave her his arm to lean on to help her to her bed. I stood in front of the curtain that separated her sleeping alcove from our communal area.

"No," said Grandma, trying to disengage herself, "don't trouble yourself. I'm fine where I am."

I blushed. The doctor saw my embarrassment and realized we all felt it. Before I could say anything to stop him, he pulled aside the curtain and entered her sleeping alcove, declaring, "A doctor goes everywhere!"

Grandma turned her head away. Soleil, Olivier (who had just come in), and I, we all bowed our heads. The doctor remained only a second in the sleeping alcove, but that was enough time for him to see… When he reappeared, he was even more embarrassed than we were, and though he didn't like emotional displays, he had to pull out his hankie. With one glance he motioned for us to meet him by the window, and I went with Soleil. The doctor grasped our hands and said in an entirely different tone of voice, "Oh, my children, my poor children…" Then, suddenly changing his tone of voice, he walked around our art studio, pointed to a canvas leaning against the wall, and said enthusiastically, "Monsieur, I'm going to buy that painting."

Soleil looked at me, astonished. It was the much-discussed canvas where he had been planning for an entire year to depict in paint that renowned feature of the sun that it cannot be looked at directly.

"But doctor," I said, "that canvas is blank."

"You can smear anything you want on it—a bunch of people, cows, little houses, I don't give a hoot, I don't even like painting. And charge me whatever you like for it."

"But doctor, that would be taking charity." I was speaking as softly as I could, but the doctor could still hear me.

He stamped his foot in anger. "Damn these Paris streets, you can't walk a single step without getting muddied by pride! Here's a young man who's haggling with me about his dignity, because I spoke disrespectfully about a masterpiece that hasn't been created yet. Who's even thinking of offending you? Who's talking about acts of charity? And even if this is one, do you have the right to refuse?" He indicated the injured woman with a quick glance. "Here, take this." And he casually extracted a 200 franc bill from his pocket and placed it on the mantle, just as nonchalantly as the emperor would take out a pinch of tobacco. Seeing my indecision, he continued, "Now, if you only want to sell your works to passionate admirers, keep your colors for yourself and take the money. I agree to preserve your… your dignity. You poor child! There's no point in twisting good intentions into something petty. Don't consider this a gift—think of it as a loan. You'll repay me in fifteen days—or in fifteen years. I'll lend it to you at ten, twenty, thirty percent interest. You can call me a usurer, that'll spare you the humiliation of showing gratitude. Monsieur, does that satisfy your pride? My own—I laugh at it. But at least," he concluded, so only I could hear, "your grandmother will no longer sleep…on the floor."

I admit that I deserved that reproach. What do you expect? When I heard him describe a painting you were going to do as mere scribbles, a painting I thought was destined to be a great work—I was hurt, but that wasn't the right time to let it show.

"Excuse me," I said to the doctor, sincerely confused, "but you don't know us, and even people in need have a right to hesitate when a stranger offers charity."

"I'm not a stranger," he replied proudly, "and any suspicion of what motivates my actions is offensive to me. I had an entirely different idea about who you were, and I regret that you didn't actually match that notion."

"Then I apologize again," I said humbly.

"Apology accepted. Let's not speak of this again," the doctor said. "But I would like to give you a bit of advice. Try to root out that little worm of vanity that's gnawing away at you. . . ." Turning to our comrades who had not heard our conversation, the doctor added, "Could I have your attention? You have to do your utmost. Since I need to come back here, I don't want to risk getting a chill. Please buy some good weather-proofing and plug all those leaks where a cold might sneak in. I'm sensitive to low temperatures. And light a fire in the hearth. Tomorrow, I hope to see a nice pot over the coals, with a chicken in it to make some bouillon for Grandma. And above all, replace what I just saw in the sleeping alcove with a decent bed. You poor woman," the doctor added, turning toward Grandma, "how did you manage to sleep there?"

"Ah, Monsieur," she answered, "I can't spend much time sleeping." Our Grandma showed her great courage with just those few simple words.

The doctor, whose superior mind included a quick intuition, understood the role she played in our household. He looked at her with an expression of real admiration, and at us with interest, no doubt, but if his farsighted glance was actually penetrating the secret of our existence, it seemed to say, "In your concern, in your expressions of tenderness, there is as much egotism as there is real love for the woman whose children you claim to be."

Ah, my brother, will everyone throw in our face this accusation of egotism? When will we be able to respond, other than with words? When will God make use of our hands to reward us for our devotion? And what if that day comes too late? If Grandma were to die before we can make her happy, think of the remorse that would cause us! Do you think we could bear it? I don't. The doctor's money, which came at exactly the right moment, allowed us to provide Grandma with all the care her condition requires. A princess would not get better treatment.

Grandma forbade us to tell our parents about her accident. She knew that Maman would want to come see her, and she dreaded the scene with our father. This almost caused quite an uproar. Maman and Papa just missed one another, because our father came to tell Grandma that he would take her back to our home. Sad to say, my brother, "our home" is one we never visit! Grandma was alone when her daughter came to see her. They were chatting very amicably when Maman heard the voice of her husband in the stairway, asking a neighbor which door was ours. She fled to the attic. When Papa arrived, he suggested to Grandma that she come to his house.

"I'm fine here," she said to him. "I have everything I need."

"So, 'their majesties,' my sons—they must be doing quite well," said our father. "Then they should rent a different place," he added, alluding to our humble lodgings. "That is, if business is that good." Before leaving, he forced Grandma to take some money, which he slipped under her bolster. "Only on the condition that my derelict sons don't get a single penny of it," he said.

After he left, a terrible scene took place between Grandma and our mother. Grandma, who had been pleasantly surprised by the visit of her son-in-law, said to Maman, "Your husband left me some money. I don't need it. Your household might miss it. Take it back." When she tried to hand our mother the money that was under the bolster, Maman gasped and started crying. Oh, my brother, I don't dare tell you why. The *money* that Papa gave us consisted of coins without value. They were foreign coins worth no more than the weight of their metal. People had given them to Papa when he wasn't paying attention, and for a long time he'd tried to find a way to slip them back into circulation. Let's not discuss this, not even with our closest friends, or even between the two of us. It's best forgotten.

All the members of our group have been wonderful with Grandma. She always has someone by her side. The very day of the accident, Lazare, the president of our group, ran over to our house to put at her disposal the funds we had set aside for communal expenses—about twenty francs. Since we were already well provided for, I just thanked him. Lazare put the money back in his pocket and asked me to lend him a small sum so he could buy some engravings he needed. With pleasure, I gave him what he asked for, letting him know that, in a case like this, he had the right to draw on the funds of our society, especially since he was the treasurer. Lazare told me that he had already made use of that resource, and he had to think of the others, not just of himself. He is working on a painting for the Salon, but I'm afraid he won't have either the time or the resources to complete it.

To return to Grandma, her condition didn't alarm us for long. The doctor came to see her every day after his lunch. He took his coffee at our home: that was the daily price of his house call. When he arrived, he joked, "Heat up my fee, and don't put too much sugar in it!" Every day we discovered a new kindness that we would never have suspected could exist in that man's violent and ill-tempered disposition. He is so prone to excess. The doctor knows now how difficult it is to climb from the street level to the seventh floor. He often is seized with misanthropic regressions to his past self. I would guess that his soul is burdened with bitter memories. He has known ingratitude. He knows our story; he accepts the spirit of our association.

When I read our charter to him, several passages made him shrug his shoulders. He said, "You young people are building on sand. Your goals are too ambitious. In groups where the goal is mutual aid, when one person starts to rise above the others, those below him can't help but wonder why they haven't succeeded at the same pace. With the ladders of camaraderie, the one with the most talent rises first, and the time comes when those on the lower rungs find their role ridiculous. It would be better if everyone got there at the same time—but that would take a miracle."

I protested against this negative and discouraging way of judging our group.

"Just wait," said the doctor. "You live in an artificial world, a world of ideas. Once you have to deal with real life, then tell me if I'm wrong. I don't want to burst your illusions, but within ten years, you all will abandon them, one by one."

While the doctor was speaking, I recalled something that confirmed his views, at least on a certain point. Remember Lazare's painting, the one he exhibited last year? Two or three of us had to stop work so Lazare could finish it in time. When the painting was in our studio, we all declared that it was magnificent. Once we saw it on display at the Salon, we didn't like it that much. The viewpoint *du jour*, you could say. And yet the painting was in the main gallery of the Salon, and so well placed that you saw it as soon as you walked in. How did it happen, then, if what the doctor said wasn't true, that two or three of our friends—especially Soleil—at first saw in this painting all the best qualities that had escaped their own work, but as soon as that canvas was displayed prominently, they wanted it relegated to an obscure nook of the Salon that would have taken three days to find. It always seemed to me that something else was at work there other than just a passing change from a favorable judgment to a critical one. This realization escaped you because you and I were the only ones whose opinion about the painting never changed.

In any case, I would gladly share volumes of gossip with you, and I enjoy so much the ways we tend to think alike, but I have to finish soon, and there are a few more details I need to communicate.

After two weeks, Grandma was feeling much better and was already starting to talk about resuming her work duties.

It took the doctor getting angry to stop her, because she was far from recovering full use of her arm. The concierge did something very inappropriate, which almost made Grandma take an action so imprudent that the consequences could have been worse than her injury. One day when we were all out of the house, the concierge gave Grandma a letter from one of the homes where she worked. The letter said that her extended absence would soon force them to replace her. Grandma had hardly finished reading the letter when she got dressed and headed out to go back to work. I arrived home right when she was walking downstairs. You should have seen the doctor when he realized that the device he had rigged for Grandma had been damaged. I thought he was going to break everything in our apartment.

I found a woman who lives on our square who will substitute for Grandma on an interim basis. That way, Grandma can keep that job, which she is very intent on, since it's one of her most lucrative.

You, too, my brother, will find we've kept a place for you, a better one than you had when you left. You'll find our lodgings much changed. It's like a hothouse here now. If you please, we even have the luxury of one of those big armchairs for the injured or convalescent which the doctor sent to us for when Grandma can get out of bed! That lazy Soleil is always curled up in it. When he's not using the armchair, Olivier claims it, and then he purrs out his elegies, which have become rather monotonous. I don't know if you feel the same as I do—his verses talk too much about things he doesn't know much about. They sometimes sound like the babblings of a precocious child. In short, I think he himself is tired of always telling the same melancholy prayer beads. In the midst of that sadness, he sometimes has wild outbursts of silliness, which show that he has a comic side, much truer than his melancholy, and that comic note is more of an echo of his true feelings than the genuine cry of a deeply broken heart. The other day, Léon told him he'd end up throwing his muse out the window and writing vaudeville sketches. Olivier was furious.

"You can say what you like," Léon answered, "you're going to do it, and you're going to become filthy rich."

One funny thing that happened, I would even say ridiculous, is that we found out Olivier and Urbain quarreled over a woman and then made peace again. Now they get together to discuss their former passion; it's as if they are collaborating on their regrets. But it was because of this affair that we ended up falling out with Urbain. Olivier is less bitter about it than the rest of us, and he's forever extending a hand in friendship to the one who betrayed him. Meanwhile Soleil, who's more in the know about these secrets than I am, assures me that Olivier detests Urbain and if he's patched things up with him it's because he wants to keep him close at hand so he can play a nasty trick on him later. I will be furious if this happens. I would prefer a lasting grudge, which would be more natural and above all, more loyal.

What other news? Oh, the landlord served us with an eviction notice right when Grandma is ill, but I had paid two installments, so he made excuses that this was purely a legal formality.

When he heard that Grandma was being treated by the premier surgeon in Paris, we rose greatly in his estimation. The landlord came all the way upstairs the other day just to get news about the convalescent. He made a "charming" comment, with the smugness that only a landlord can have: "I didn't realize my building was so tall," he said to us. No doubt because of all our new embellishments, he found our apartment more pleasant and better arranged that he'd thought. I just hope that doesn't inspire him to raise our rent! It's dangerous for renters to make improvements to an apartment. The landlord always thinks he's the one to thank, and wants to profit from them at the expense of the tenants. When he was leaving, he told me he might have work for me. Does he want me to give his stairway a fresh coat of paint?

When you return, you'll find many little things we didn't have when you were here—among others, a good lamp that we bought with you in mind. We've gone ahead and purchased several things we greatly needed which seem like luxuries to us. If you only knew how strange it felt to buy them! For so long, we did exactly the opposite. As soon as you get back, you should begin work on the painting for the doctor. I first thought about a copy of Rembrandt's *The Good Samaritan;* that would have been very apropos.

I took the doctor to the Louvre so he could choose which painting he wanted you to copy. His opinion about Rembrandt was quite curious. I showed the doctor two or three canvases where that master so powerfully reveals his luminous genius. The doctor was not used to discerning shapes in bitumen shadows where only the center is in bright light. He exclaimed, "Bah! Always the same thing. A cave someone has thrown a bomb into!" After we made the rounds of all the galleries, the doctor, who had started to trust the taste of his guide, then decided on a painting by François Boucher in the gallery of French art: according to the guidebook, it's called *Fauns and Bacchantes Playing among the Vines.* "And look, no fig leaves!" the doctor pointed out, laughing heartily. "That's the one I'd like a copy of!" What will your serious paintbrush do with all that fluff?

Now I am really bidding you adieu, that is, till we see each other again. We're hoping that will be in two weeks' time, at the latest. Some of our group need your advice about what pieces to submit for the exhibition. There is talk about fine things glimpsed in the studios of some young people who are still unknown. So much the better, a thousand times better for them, and good luck to the new arrivals. Success is contagious. I'm sending you kisses from Grandma. She has just fallen asleep in her big armchair, her rosary in her hands. On her lips, there is a prayer for us: may God hear her! Poor sainted woman! Just think that her best time may be one where she has suffered so much.

Adieu, from your brother in the brotherhood,

Paul

P.S.: Just as I was finishing this letter, I received one from the doctor. He has found me a student among his clients, a very rich woman from another country who has arrived in Paris to spend the winter. A fall from a horse has consigned her dainty foot to the care of our good doctor. Tomorrow I'll go to visit this woman in her convalescence.

III. The Procession

Francis read this long letter several times. The words introduced him to a life he had caught only a few vague and cloudy glimpses of previously. This time, it was as clear as a report of facts in a legal proceeding. All these sad scenes passed before his eyes, and when the narrator's pen had hesitated to include certain details, Francis added them with a shudder in his thoughts. What a difference between his own worst days and those of the Man with the Glove and his friends. And yet those young people seemed to accept their destiny as if it was something required of them. To achieve the goal they set for themselves, they could take only one path, and they followed it tranquilly, just as when you travel you accept the dangers inherent in a particular route you know is risky. No recriminations, no complaints that frighten you and sow discouragement, hardly even an appeal to divine providence. Instead, a courage that was even-tempered and with a patient faith in a shared future.

Francis, on the other hand, had just experienced a few privations and had undergone some minor struggles with hardship, and how deeply he lamented, how much he groaned about the bitterness of his fate! How skillfully his vanity constructed a pedestal for himself every time he endured any kind of setback! How his courage, so quickly short of breath, forgot that you don't soften obstacles, you break through them!

After a deadly battle, a soldier found again a brother in arms he'd lost sight of in the heat of combat; still shaken by the dangers he'd braved, proud of a wound he'd received in full view of his commanding officers, he said to his comrade, "So, in the end, you didn't fight, did you? We didn't see you in the line of fire." "I was in the smoke," answered the other soldier, who revealed a large wound in his chest, stretched out his arms, closed his eyes, and fell. That's not so different from those who fight while concealed by the smoke of life's battles, anonymous heroes no one mourns when their fate runs its course. For them, the gravedigger shovels a plot without even knowing what name to inscribe on their cross.

After he finished reading, the sympathetic curiosity that had pushed Francis to grab the letter turned into passionate admiration. His enthusiasm was so exaggerated that he saw that group of unknown artists as larger than life. The next morning, Francis went to the Louvre early in order to be among the first in the door. He placed the letter back where he'd found it. He had promised himself that he would get his neighbor to open up to him, and not to let another day slip by without becoming friends with that young man. His plan was in vain that day, though: the Man with the Glove did not appear in the gallery. Around midday, the same young man who had brought the piece of bread came to take away the easel, the stool, and everything else that belonged to Francis' neighbor. When Francis summoned the courage to ask him if his friend was ever coming back to the Louvre, the young man said that *his brother* was not going to be there for some time. He nodded to Francis, and then left.

That night, after finding his friends, Francis described for them the Man with the Glove and asked if any of them by chance knew him, without revealing any of the information he'd already obtained. One of Francis' comrades declared that he knew nothing personal about the young man in question, but that they were supposed to have been rivals in a competition at their art school, and he only knew that the other student had almost joined a freemason lodge. That jogged the memory of one of Francis' other friends, who told him that the young man he was talking about had worked for a while in the studio of a member of the Institut de France, sponsor of the Académie des Beaux-Arts. He had been sent away because he fought a duel with a young man from a good family who frequented the studio, a dilettante who had made a joke about one of the Man with the Glove's relatives, either an elderly aunt or a grandmother.

A third friend then remembered that the man in question was named Antoine, and that, along with his brother, he was the founder and most influential member of a little club that the members called the Water Drinkers. "They think of themselves as a sort of artistic freemasonry," he continued, not without irony. "It's quite hard to get admitted to the group. They subject you to extremely difficult tests, considering they live in such poverty. If you're a painter, first you have to improvise a masterpiece like *The Transfiguration* in only twenty-five minutes. And if you're a sculptor, a group like Cellini's Perseus and Medusa. If you're a poet, a poem like *The Iliad.* Once you've passed that test, they put your application to a vote. If you're admitted, you take all sorts of oaths that you swear on paintbrushes, pens, and chisels, all arranged in a cross. Since genius is a faculty of divine origin, you have to swear never to profane it by surrendering to brute commercialism. To put it plainly, they forbid you ever to make money on your art. The initiation ceremony ends with drinking a large glass of water that you have to down in one gulp. That's their ingenious symbol for a society where the members only drink water, and never wine."

This grotesque summary seemed to Francis a parody of the serious ideas forming the basis of that society. What he'd just learned, added to what he already knew, only sharpened his desire to meet the Water Drinkers. The idealized view Francis had of this group made him think that the members of this church of the arts all had great talent. That meant they'd only admit to their ranks someone who seemed to them to be their equal. His friends' fleeting judgments of this group had an effect on him, of course. But while they were expressing their admiration for it, Francis asked himself, *What would the Man with the Glove and his friends think of me? Would they consider me worthy of membership in their society?*

It sometimes happens that an artist picks out from the crowd a group, or even sometimes an isolated individual, whose opinion counts more for him more than that of the multitudes, just as the ancients drank toasts to unknown gods. A certain artist begins a work as a kind of sacred offering to a friend who is not even aware of it. Then, when the work is unveiled to the public, it's rare that the one it was dedicated to does not stop in front of it, suddenly seized by a mysterious voice that says, "You don't recognize me? In all this crowd that surrounds me, it's your glance I was waiting for, it's your approval I want." And if that admired one stops, if he looks, if he approves, then at that same moment his approval is sensed, magnetically guessed by the one who was waiting for it as a reward for his past, and an encouragement for his future.

Whether or not he actually gave credence to these mystical messages, these currents that allow isolated and like-minded individuals to communicate, Francis acted as if he did believe in them. We've discussed the minor success his paintings had, and the rumblings that were starting to increase his reputation. They surpassed his expectations. And because they gave him renewed courage, he immediately told himself that the Water Drinkers would one day be proud to admit him to their ranks. Other than Francis' growing reputation, nothing else about this assumption was very realistic. Those starting out in a particular branch of the arts don't think much of those who are already working in it, or those who succeed. The ones practicing that art have already made their niche—and they defend it. But for the beginners who have not yet made a name for themselves, their real interest is in the number of competitors that every day grows larger, and above all, how they rate in comparison to their newest rival. This can easily be verified by the rush that all young artists are in to view the work of a colleague exhibiting for the first time. This nervous curiosity is hardly blameworthy. Each struggle is interesting when an artist faces the public for the first time. Whether the result is success or failure, everyone holds their breath to see the verdict of that supreme judge. If the judge condemns, the spectators calmly trickle away, some siding with the defeated party, others against, while most remain indifferent. "Well, man overboard!" they say, philosophically. If, on the other hand, the artist succeeds, the multitude moves in his direction like an ant colony stirred by the random poke of a cane.

Despite how limited Francis' first attempt at exhibiting before the public was, and how restrained the echo was in response, all the would-be artists of Paris gathered in front of the window where his paintings were displayed. A few of them, who knew the dealer, went inside to examine the canvases more closely and to gather information about their creator. Was he young? Was he rich? Who did he study with? Wasn't he an amateur artist of the sort you sometimes meet in society, a celebrity of the salons, whose head has been turned by sketchbook triumphs and the applause of white-gloved hands, and who has just on a whim waged a campaign in the domain of the arts, the same way a dandy would take Baden by storm, and who says to the public, "*Mon Dieu,* it's just a mere trifle I did to amuse myself. But what do you think of it? Tell me the truth, but keep in mind, I'm not a professional." To which the public often responds, with the requested honesty: *It shows.*

The dealer, interrogated about Francis, said just who he was, but with much exaggeration. "And you think you're poor, you jokers!" he said. "Grouse all you like against fate and the public. The public doesn't even know what it wants! It wants you to please it, to satisfy it, to surpass its wildest fantasies, but do not, as you do three-quarters of the time, satisfy your own fantasies, which the public cares nothing for. Every purse that jingles is demanding, and has the right to be. Make concessions to the public, sacrifice to the taste of the day, without worrying if it will be tomorrow's taste. If you do that, you'll find me a useful go-between, forgiving and devoted. I'll get your work out there. You'll have a well-stocked and well-located establishment. We'll spruce up your canvas in a pretty frame, we'll put it on a handsome easel, and we'll display it to all comers in the bright glare of four gaslights."

"Thank you very much for the gilded frames, your elegant gallery, and the light from your gaslights," an artist replied. "They come at too great a cost. I'd prefer just a wall to show my art, and my freedom."

"Yes, but museum directors don't pay an advance," the art dealer said, "and the jury doesn't always award you a nail at the Salon. Unless you happen to be Monsieur La-dee-dah, the crowds at the Salon don't look for you, because they have no idea who you are. If by chance they happen to see you, and on an impulse they decide to buy your work, it might happen that they don't make the purchase right when the thought strikes them, and then they forget all about their whim while picking up their cane at the coat check, and if they happen to run into a friend in the street, they say nothing more than, 'I saw something fairly nice.' 'Who was it by?' asks the friend. 'A certain Monsieur…Oh, well, I already forgot his name.'"

"That's all public exhibitions are good for," continued the dealer. "In my gallery, I do things differently. I talk up the paintings, I tell heartwarming stories about the canvases, I insinuate to the collector that by buying a beautiful work of art, he himself will be able to make a good one. I have a saying that I live by: Painting seen, painting sold. But you have to know how to do it, when to turn up the heat, and when to turn it down. I know the art of fitting the shoe to the customer; or like they say, I know how to hook a fish, and when a collector comes into my shop and sits down in one of my armchairs and looks at a painting, I go to my desk and jot a note to the artist saying the sale is already in the bag. Mount another canvas and get to work."

Meanwhile, Francis had heard that his debut as an artist was being talked about in Paris studios and academies, so he assumed that the Water Drinkers already knew of him. By now, they must have formed an opinion of him. What was that opinion? He would have given half of his success to know. Hoping that the Man with the Glove had resumed his work in the Louvre, and realizing that if he went about it in the right way he might learn what the Water Drinkers thought of his work, Francis paced from gallery to gallery in the Louvre, but he didn't find the man he was looking for. He questioned all the museum regulars, he even asked the guards, but no one was able to give him any information.

One day, walking on the quais along the Seine, Francis had to wait while a funeral procession passed by. He realized it must be for a famous person because it included mourners of all social classes, and in particular, distinguished members of the Faculty of Medicine. The demeanor of the cortege was silent and reverential. This was no common man that the horse-drawn hearse was carrying to his final resting place. This had to be a person whose name would be known well beyond the time when it had been erased from his tombstone, because his funeral had the air of a triumphant march toward posterity. The looks on the faces of those in the funeral procession indicated that the loss of this individual was a cause for widespread mourning. Francis was going to ask whose burial this was, and then struck his forehead like a man who had just realized something obvious. At the back of the procession following the cortege, he saw an isolated group, and in the middle of it walked the Man with the Glove. On his arm was an elderly woman wearing garments that were plainer than plain. Another young man, whom Francis realized must be the brother Paul, also helped support the poor woman. Those three figures, who were the only ones not dressed in the color of grief, had wrapped a band of black crepe around their left arms as a sign of mourning. Behind them walked five or six other young people, their heads bare and with solemn expressions. Francis realized he was witnessing the funeral of Doctor ***, whose death he had read about in the newspaper, and he understood that the young men accompanying the two brothers and their grandmother were the other members of the Water Drinkers. Francis removed his hat, stepped out into the street, and began walking at the rear of the funeral procession, without anyone noticing his presence.

The procession reached the Rue de la Roquette, which led to Père Lachaise Cemetery. When they began to pass stores that sold marble headstones and funerary ornaments, businesses that were very numerous at the outskirts of the necropolis, the Man with the Glove, who from now on we will refer to by his real name, Antoine, left his grandmother on the arm of his brother Paul and went to speak with his other friends. Even though Francis was only a couple of steps behind him, Antoine did not notice him. Antoine had a short conversation with the Water Drinkers, after which each of them dug into their pockets. Once they had put together a collection, Antoine broke away, and Francis saw him enter the shop of a gravestone maker. A few moments later, Antoine took his place again next to his grandmother. In his hand he had a large wreath of the dried flowers they call everlastings. The poor woman looked astonished, but her grandson whispered a few words to her, and the old woman smiled sadly in gratitude to the Water Drinkers.

While they were entering Père Lachaise Cemetery, the rain, which had been threatening earlier in the day, started to pour heavily. Despite the inclement weather, the full ceremony took place. All funerary honors were accorded to this illustrious man that the earth was about to reclaim. The Water Drinkers and the grandmother pushed their way through the crowd and took their places right by the graveside, where beautiful words were spoken by the same medical colleagues who had been the doctor's rivals during his lifetime, because where death begins, justice begins as well.

A renowned orator gave a eulogy, retracing the doctor's distinguished career and his full life. Above all, the speaker endeavored to recall for the assembled listeners the high moral character of the deceased. After the orator described the doctor's eminence, he also described his humanity. He showed how the doctor had walked the sacred paths of charity. The orator spoke about all the public service the doctor had performed during his lifetime. Then the speaker evoked another figure, a somber Lazarus of the people, a living symbol of eternal poverty and suffering, and described a hovel with only a straw pallet where sunlight never enters, a patient who knows no hope; the speaker showed the patient, when the next morning dawned, throwing open the curtain of his sleeping alcove and calling in a pained voice for the doctor whose words had given him such courage, a doctor who now could no longer respond. The orator also sketched the many good works the doctor had done, even in a lifetime cut short; he opened up the garrets of the working class neighborhoods and showed the worker covering with black crepe his tools that put bread in the mouths of his children, tools that the scientific knowledge of the great practitioner had restored to his hands.

In the midst of this discourse that seemed to come from lips touched by the sacred embers of the alchemists, an apparition appeared to manifest itself out of the very words of his speech and attracted the glance of the orator, at the same time that it also drew the attention of the listeners. An elderly woman, who had already been sobbing for a while, succeeded in breaking free of the two young men who were restraining her. Advancing to the bare earth around the open grave, she placed the wreath of everlastings over the temporary cross that had already been planted at the head of the burial site, and with her garments dripping with rain, she fell on her knees before the grave in a puddle of mud, put her hands together, and prayed.

"Gentlemen," said the orator to the spectators who were already overcome with emotion, "anything more I could say would mean less than these tears, this crown, this prayer! Let us follow this woman's example. On your knees, and let us pray with her."

That illustrious orator, bowing his head, made a gesture with his hand, and the entire crowd obeyed. It was a striking moment, and everyone seemed moved by it, Francis as much as the others.

Antoine and Paul were about to join their grandmother in her act of gratitude, but the brothers were distracted by a short conversation they overheard. Once the orator had finished his eulogy, he rejoined the group of mourners and stood next to a person who seemed to be waiting for his instructions. That person was the stenographer assigned to transcribe the funeral oration for a newspaper.

"So dramatic, and you staged that so well!" the young man enthused to the orator.

"Absolutely," said the orator, "except I actually had no idea the woman was going to do that. In fact, what she did made me cut the last paragraph of my speech, my summation. I'd be upset if you didn't print it. Take this page, and add it to your transcript." The stenographer accepted the paper, thanked the orator, and slipped away.

That revelation was a slap in the face to the brothers, and an insult to their grief. It was as if their grandmother was being used as an extra in a scene from a play about a funeral. So it could happen that hallowed ground could compete for dramatic effect with the stage of a theater! Antoine and Paul exchanged sad glances. In each other's blushes they recognized the stigmata of the same insult. The two of them stepped out of the circle of mourners and walked up to their grandmother, who was still on her knees.

"Get up," said Paul to her, his voice trembling with emotion. "You're making a spectacle of yourself."

"And of all us," added Antoine, trying to pull her up to a standing position.

The old woman looked at her grandsons in astonishment. She saw their upset faces, still red with shame. Anger seemed to be burning on their lips. *Is it really my children looking at me like that?* her eyes seemed to say, still full of tears.

"Don't you see everyone's staring at us?" said Paul.

"What do they think of us?" asked Antoine, looking furiously at the spectators.

"I came here to be seen," murmured the old woman. "You're afraid people are looking at us, you're blushing, you're ashamed, shaking. It's as if you'd been caught doing something bad."

A terrible realization flashed across her eyes like a lightning bolt, causing her to stop crying. "Stand back," she said, gesturing toward her grandsons. "I understand you.... Poor man," she said, looking down into the grave, "forgive me for not finishing my prayer. My grandsons interrupted me because my gratitude shames them. You said it well, my good Samaritan, their miserable pride has killed all the good in them. Your gifts are still warm in their hands, and already they've forgotten you."

"Grandma," cried Antoine, "if you only knew..."

"What I know is that your hats are still on your heads in front of this freshly dug grave." With a sudden gesture, she ripped the black crepe from the arms of her grandchildren and hurled the tatters away, saying in a choking voice, "Take these off, my sons. It's enough to be ungrateful without also lying. *Mon Dieu, Mon*

Dieu," she cried, "you've cursed my old age. You've heaped sorrow on my sorrow. My children who I loved so, they're ingrates! You've broken my heart," she added weakly.

Meanwhile the crowd began to disperse. The grandmother and her grandsons were alone in their solitude. Antoine and Paul explained why they had acted the way they did. The grandmother heard them and her face regained some of its serenity in hearing how ardently they defended themselves against the accusation of ingratitude. But her soul had difficulty understanding the pride they couldn't suppress. She would have liked her grandchildren to be self-effacing, to deny the sense of honor that had distracted them from their grief. Still, her tender heart felt the sorrow she had caused her grandsons, and she started to apologize, but they closed her lips with a gentle gesture. They rejoined the Water Drinkers who had stood off to the side, and together they began to walk home.

Francis, concealed by his umbrella, walked close by, pretending he was trying to find his way home. He waited till the Water Drinkers passed in front of him. Antoine was at the very back of the group, talking with one of his friends, while Paul and the grandmother were at the front. It was now raining twice as hard, and the drenched ground made their progress extremely difficult. Francis almost bumped into Antoine, so Antoine couldn't help seeing and recognizing him. The moment was not at all conducive to a friendly conversation, in several respects. But Francis didn't have the luxury of choosing his moment, so he decided to make the best of it. Greeted rather coldly by Antoine, who hadn't really noticed him during the procession or the burial, Francis had difficulty connecting one word to another as they were leaving the cemetery. They spoke, but said nothing meaningful. At the exit, the coachmen who waited for fares on the boulevard, seeing a group arriving, assumed they were going to be flagged down, but the group passed right by the hansom cabs without stopping.

“What a shame that Grandma can’t stand the jostling of a carriage,” said Antoine, as if to answer Francis’ astonishment at seeing the Water Drinkers continue on foot. And the rain was not letting up. Francis suffered greatly to see that elderly woman exposed to a glacial downpour. He knew exactly how to interpret Antoine’s excuses for not taking a carriage.

“Monsieur, please take my umbrella,” Francis offered assertively, “and hold it over your grandmother till you get back home.” Antoine tried to refuse, but Francis insisted in such a cordial and unaffected manner that Antoine ended up accepting, and he thanked Francis profusely. Antoine brought the umbrella over to his grandmother, who turned around to thank the donor. Francis respectfully bowed his head.

“But you, Monsieur,” said Antoine, rejoining Francis, “you’ll have no protection from the rain…”

“No worries, I’m young,” responded Francis. He was going to say, *and well dressed for rain,* but he thought better of it.

“How can I return your umbrella?” asked Antoine.

“Here’s my address.” Francis took a card out of his wallet and gave it to Antoine. Francis thought Antoine would read it and react to his name, but Antoine just shoved the card in his pocket and repeated his thanks.

They had arrived at the Place de la Bastille. Francis explained that this was his destination. He saluted the others, bowed respectfully to the grandmother, and crossed to the side of the street opposite the Water Drinkers.

IV. The Water Drinkers

As soon as Francis returned home, he began to rearrange his studio. He knew that in any first encounter designed with a specific purpose in mind, the surroundings are crucial. He felt that a personal connection would be more difficult to make if Antoine's first thought on entering his home would be to compare it to his own in a way that greatly favored Francis. So Francis hid all of his recent purchases that gave the impression that his studio was too well furnished; he concealed the splurges he had made that were unrelated to his work; he took down from the walls his half-finished canvases that even he knew were not good; and finally he moved to spots with better lighting his paintings that he thought would attract a compliment. After an hour's work, any evidence of these meticulous preparations or his domestic comforts had disappeared. Francis calculated that this carefully designed set would prove to his guest that their ways of life were similar, so that Francis would form a bond with Antoine.

The next morning, Antoine arrived as arranged. Francis had taken his place on stage, as they say in the theater. Antoine gave Francis' studio a quick glance, and he seemed to approve. The first quarter of an hour was taken up with small talk, but since Antoine was in the studio of a fellow artist, politeness required him to take notice of the works that were right in front of his eyes. Antoine did as custom dictated, particularly since there was a canvas on an easel placed so clearly in plain sight that it was obvious it was meant to be discussed. Antoine intelligently praised what he saw. When he noticed a defect, he pointed it out, as if to give more weight to the qualities he praised. But Francis could sense in his words a note of discomfort and a slight hesitation.

Francis had no illusions about his visitor. He knew Antoine's attention to his work was merely a way of was repaying him for the minor service that Francis had rendered. *His feet are burning to leave here and run down those stairs,* Francis thought. *If I had a clock, he'd be glancing at it.* What astonished him, though, was that Antoine didn't even mention the paintings that Francis had recently exhibited. In all the arts, young people who begin to produce are under the impression that everyone must know their work, and that there's a universal preoccupation with them. They also consider that silence about their work equates to the harshest criticism, and that ignorance of their art is an insult. Not willing to admit that Antoine simply did not know his paintings, Francis concluded that if Antoine did not take this occasion to praise him, it was because he had a negative opinion of him, and Francis thought that the Water Drinkers, represented in this instance by Antoine, must be very picky indeed.

They managed to get out of this thorny situation when Francis skillfully steered the conversation to a master artist they both knew. Francis deliberately criticized that artist with exaggerated vehemence. When he saw how forcefully Antoine responded to this, he realized he had touched a sore spot, and that Antoine, who was making a sort of official visit to a stranger with the goal of their remaining strangers, had finally unveiled some of his true self. Antoine could not see his idols tarnished without rushing to their defense, and he could not have a conversation about art without becoming passionate. Once Antoine got carried away, his open nature broke through his reserve, and his whole personality revealed itself, not just as an artist, but as a man. When he saw that his visitor was now talking freely, Francis revealed a hidden closet, took out two logs, and lit a fire in the wood-burning stove.

"You actually have wood?" Antoine asked naively.

"I have a model coming this whole week, and since I just sold a couple of paintings, I bought supplies for heat."

"So we're going to talk like two bourgeois, with our backs to the fire?"

"We might as well act out the old proverb: *Backs to the fire, belly on the table*, and also have something to eat."

"But..." Antoine objected, embarrassed.

"What's the matter?" asked Francis, smiling. "Don't stand on ceremony. You probably haven't eaten anything this morning, and neither have I. It's much more pleasant to have company for lunch."

Antoine didn't have a reason to refuse, and he had one very pressing reason to accept.

Excellent, Francis said to himself. *If we haven't broken the ice yet, at least we've started to chip away at it.*

Francis opened the window and hailed the doorman to order food. A quarter of an hour later they were acting out that old bourgeois proverb, which for a starving artist was next door to utopia. Behind them, the stove was practically roaring, and in front of them, the table was set. Their interrupted conversation resumed, even more animatedly. The two friends—they were already calling each other that—were still chatting away when night descended.

"And now," said Francis, "how about a nice dinner? I hope you'll also be my guest this evening." One word from Antoine would confirm how friendly they had already become.

Seeing that Francis was planning to take him out to an elegant restaurant, Antoine stopped Francis at the threshold of his studio and said, "You're about to do something very foolish, and I'm not going to be your accomplice. It's going to cost you at least twenty francs for us to sit for an hour in a beautiful dining room where we won't even feel comfortable speaking, especially not about the things we really need to discuss."

"Don't be ridiculous!" said Francis.

"No, it's true," Antoine continued, "and to be honest, it would be uncomfortable for me to sit and eat there while everyone at my home is going hungry. Let's go instead to a modest establishment. On the way there, we'll pass by my house and I'll give my brother a few sous that you'll lend me. I'll pay you back tomorrow, when I'm due to be paid for a month of art lessons."

"We'll do better than that," suggested Francis. "Invite your brother and your friends to join us, if they're at your house."

"Not possible. It would make you uncomfortable, and them, too. Once I introduce you to the group, we'll see. Not to mention, my brother wants to work this evening. If he has something to eat and a few hours' worth of heat, light, and tobacco, you'll have done him a great service."

Francis slipped a gold coin into Antoine's palm right before they reached the Water Drinkers' doorway. "Give me five minutes," said Antoine. While Francis was walking up and down the block, he noticed Antoine's brother leaving the house, accompanied by one of the young men who had been part of the funeral procession. Shortly afterwards, Francis saw the two of them return. One of them was carrying a bundle of firewood on his back, and the other had a loaf of bread tucked under his arm. Francis waited at a distance so they wouldn't recognize him.

Five minutes after that, Antoine came back downstairs. "Follow me," he said to Francis.

Antoine led him to a sort of brasserie. If the meal went on for a while, it wasn't because of the food: Antoine refused to order anything more than the minimum. As they were getting up to leave, Francis was shocked that Antoine paid the waiter for the bill. "What are you doing?" he said.

"Just let it be," said Antoine. When they were in the street, Antoine added, "Here's your change," and handed him what was left of the gold coin.

After he subtracted the cost of the dinner, Francis calculated that the Water Drinkers had only used two francs of the twenty-franc value of the coin. "I don't think you understood what I was saying earlier," Francis said reproachfully.

"You're the one who doesn't understand," Antoine replied. "I only asked for a few sous."

"But since it's no trouble to me…"

"But it would trouble *us*!" Antoine answered in a manner that made it clear that he would not look kindly on Francis insisting. And when Francis still seemed about to object, Antoine added, "Listen, there is a reason for what I'm doing. You saw how freely I acted around you. We're on much better terms than we could have imagined this morning. That transition happened quickly, but that speed is a testimony to the openness that has joined our hands in friendship. Time will tell what develops between us. Time does for friendships what it does for wines: they lose their dryness and acidity as they age, which allows us to appreciate their best qualities. Once we get to know one another, we'll shed the little doubts and fears that go along with the first steps of friendship. And now my friend, since it seems very important to you, as it is to me, let's go have a look at your paintings. I should have gone to see them sooner, if I'd had an occasion to be in that quarter of Paris, because my brother described them to me as…noteworthy."

They arrived at Morin's gallery. Antoine examined the paintings and at first he found them quite exciting. But then he began to study the canvases with a more serious eye.

"So, what do you think of my debut?" asked Francis.

"I can't praise your work based on these paintings," Antoine answered. "They surprised me at first, but these two canvases don't stand up to closer scrutiny. The most striking parts at first seem very good, but they're only skillful parodies of the masters you've studied with. You've fallen into the old trap set by art teachers. When I saw your other paintings earlier, I wondered if you were getting ready to create another tour de force, and if you were actually able to summon that ability at will. I'm going to tell you something that might surprise you. I hope you *don't* have that ability, and that your first efforts are limited to fumbling in the dark, and to trial and error—in other words, to study. That's how you find your way, when your progress is the result of research, and not just chance. That's when you get lasting results you can apply usefully and seriously. Yes, I know you're going to answer that feeling and inspiration can take the place of study; but inspiration, when it comes at the start of a career, is often mixed with naïveté. Under those circumstances, inspiration is impatient and can't wait till it's ripened through the hard work of the artist. It's a diamond that won't wait for the gem cutter. But that's not your story. You're not naïve, because your painting is full of gimmicks. You're not original, because one can sense in your work—maybe despite your best intentions—that you're preoccupied with influences outside your own process. These paintings aren't produced by inspiration, or we would have seen that in your earlier works. What are they, then? An accident. And that accident will only be a lucky one if you make something of it from here."

Francis kept silent. He seemed only half convinced, so Antoine continued.

"I'm not denying that Morin sees in your almost-realized art something that could make him a small fortune," Antoine said. "He wants to turn you into the same thing he's made of others. He'll make you produce a lot. He'll maintain you in a state of what seems like well-being, a state you certainly could not achieve if you broke with him. He has connections that will bring you success, and that will allow him to attach a commercial value to your name. That's his business. He'll launch you in a world that is to the real world what his merchandise is to real art. If at some point you refuse to keep producing at his pace, he'll hang up a hammock for you to laze around in, confidant that in no time you'll be back at his cash register asking for more. Then that kind, indulgent friend will disappear. You'll find yourself face-to-face with a dealer who shows you his books to prove that you're taking up too much space in the debit column, and that it's time to correct the balance. The days when you could make do with very little, often with nothing—those will be far behind you; you'll develop expensive tastes, your self-esteem will be used to being well-fed and you'll become accustomed to insipid praise that makes you blush, but which fake artists need in order to keep working, just like mules get excited by the sound of their bells and keep trudging forward. You'll be treated with indifference by your fellow artists who will consider your reputation a meaningless craze; you'll speak of *their* work the way a snake spews venom; you'll get your revenge on them by saying that even one of your paintings brings in more than they earn in a year from their labors. In order to restore the balance in your account with Morin, you'll agree to keep producing; and Morin, who now has you under his thumb, will no longer give you the freedom to indulge you whims. He'll say to you: I don't want this, I want that. He'll write the plan for each of your paintings in the corner of the canvas. Then one fine day, when he's bled you dry, he'll tell you that you're slipping, he'll rub in your face the success of his new recruits, who in time will suffer the same fate as you, and in the end, he'll say he's giving you your freedom, unless you happen to want to grind pigments in his art factory. You'll try to make do without him, but you'll find out you're constantly fighting yourself. You will be excluded precisely because your reputation has been compromised. You'll rediscover your passion for serious study; but art, which is a jealous lover, will confine you to ranks of the lowest traders in second-hand goods. Your work will end up in the grasp of the auctioneers, and will be sold off between a heap of iron and bags stuffed with rags. What will you do then, discouraged, disdained, contemptible, too far along in your career to start over, pitied by those who knew you before, when they were the ones who were poor and obscure, but who now are happy and successful, possessing in reality what you only grasped the shadow of, while you're reduced to painting the stations of the cross at one hundred francs the dozen for factories that supply small-town churches?"

These alarming prognostications did not persuade Francis. "But, Antoine," he said, "I still have to live."

"Didn't you live before you met Morin?" Antoine volleyed.

"Of course," Francis said, "but not without suffering. I don't know how I could go back to that life. And yet," he went on, "If I had moral support, the encouragement and the example of my peers, if I lived—the way you do—surrounded by enthusiastic friends with all the camaraderie that your group shares, if I were in continual contact with kindred spirits, I might find the faith I'm missing now. I do miss that. I might discover the kind of perseverance that can resist seductions. But now I'm isolated. I had friends, but they've distanced themselves from me; I'm terrified of solitude and boredom. I wonder if you can understand that."

"Perfectly," answered Antoine. "You would have to join our group. Is that what you're asking me? You probably heard about our little meetings, and all the taunts that, God knows, have rained down on us. It's easy to bad-mouth what you don't know. If our association matches the hope that you have for it, my friends and I will try to save you. But you have to know what you're getting into if you join us."

Antoine then explained in detail to Francis the mysteries of an existence that he had only glimpsed. He gave a short description of each of his friends. Antoine said that not all of them had as yet proven they had real talent: "We have poets whose muse is still stuttering, but stuttering truth. There are some who've already produced notable works. As for our poverty, we accept it the way we accept the cold in winter, but our winter is harsh, I admit. For us, Hope is not an allegorical figure; it's a constant companion, malnourished maybe, and sighing its consolations, instead of singing them. Some people tell us that the life we lead is good for young people: character steeps in it, like tea in a pot."

"Or like wine turning to vinegar?" asked Francis.

"We've tried to escape the bitterness that consumes some of the most talented people, the ones who turn against their own hardships. If we've succeeded, it's only because of the example of sacrifice in our midst: I'm talking about our grandmother.

"I'll tell you her story in a few words," said Antoine. "I think you'll admire the role she plays in our household. Three years ago, she lived with our parents. She'd completed her years of labor and was enjoying the rest and tranquility of old age, like someone who's finished a good day's work. Since my brother and I didn't want to live the life our father had in mind for us, one evening we told our father we were going to start work in a painter's studio. As soon as we'd finished dinner, he said, 'You've eaten my bread for the very last time. Go and live somewhere else. Start packing your trunks.' 'Then I'm packing mine, too,' said our grandmother, getting up from the table. 'I'm leaving with my grandchildren.' Our mother started to cry, but Grandma remained calm. She went upstairs to her room, quickly bundled up the few rags she owned, and caught up with us as we were leaving the threshold of our paternal home, never to return. Why we were leaving, where we were going, what all this fuss about art was—that, she didn't understand. What she did grasp was that we were going to be alone in the world, and that we were young and not very well prepared to live on our own. How could we reject such tenderness? How could we make her understand that she might be a burden to us, and how precarious our exile might be?

"In fact, we were the ones who didn't understand," Antoine continued. "Two days after we'd moved into our first studio, we saw the true devotion of that heroic soul. Grandma had gone out looking for work, and she'd found some. Her years showed on her, but you know that giant Antaeus in Greek mythology whose strength was renewed just by touching the earth? Well, as in the myth, that hardworking woman found new strength when she started a new job. 'My poor children,' she said, 'you've chosen a profession that brings in nothing, but if it's what you really want, that's the most important thing. I know one type of work that's within reach of anyone with arms, and it will help us to live. When you start earning money from your art and you realize your dreams, you'll buy me a big armchair. I'll sit in it and never get up, and I'll die happy seeing your joy.'

"We wanted to keep her from working and to make her move back with our parents, but our pleading fell on deaf ears. She silenced us with only a few words: 'Does it make you blush to see your grandmother working in other people's homes?' What could we say, other than to accept her devotion?

"During the eighteen months after we left our father's home, it was that woman, twice as old as my brother and I put together, who supported us with her earnings. Even now, if we didn't have the support of her two arms, we might have to make compromises that would be lethal for our art. In a word, we'd also have to seek out the protection of a Morin. But avoiding compromises of that sort is the very heart of our group. Each one of us has his own specialty and refuses to do anything else than what he was put on earth for, and each waits patiently to create the works that will announce their art has arrived, once we've acquired all the necessary abilities and strengths. There are those among us who are already in a position to benefit financially from their work, and that could provide some relief not only for themselves, but for all of us. In our family nothing belongs just to one person, everything that comes in is shared. But the others, who haven't yet made a name for themselves, they're at the mercy of foolish pretentions and advice that goes against their way of thinking, so they prefer to maintain their integrity and wait for their day to come. Some accuse us of having a cynical pride. Our pride isn't as foolish as some might think. We will accept any protection freely offered to us, from whoever gives it; and we would welcome all sympathy that looks past appearances to the core of who we are and doesn't demand servile gratitude from us, or words we find offensive. We bend naturally to the necessities of a difficult life, but we refuse to bend to a morality that's easier to act on than to justify. We're not extreme puritans, and we would gladly exchange our life for a better one, so long as that metamorphosis doesn't involve abandoning our ideas about art. We are men and we are young; to be sequestered from the normal pleasures and joys of our age often causes us pain; we know the assaults of temptations, but we push them back, and since we don't find our pleasures and joys elsewhere, we get them from our work."

When he saw that Francis was listening with great interest, Antoine wanted to answer all the objections that had been made to the Water Drinkers. "They accuse us of being self-serving," he continued, "because we let our grandmother work, and she's elderly, but her big heart gives the lie to those allegations. She knows that her devotion is building a foundation for our future, and her face radiates with pride when she sees the courage we draw from her. We all help one another, every way we can. A year ago, I wanted to take a trip to do studies based on nature. Each of my friends did without something as a sort of tax, and they collected the funds to pay for my voyage. We're as honest as anyone can be with one another, and never two-faced. The mood among us is as even-tempered and happy as can be, because sadness is useless, and one of our principles is that whatever is useless is harmful.

"Of course we have flaws, but we've decided to live on good terms with one another, instead of quarreling and criticizing one another. We respect all opinions about art, even if they contradict ours. Our families look on our lives as the worst sort of chaos, and they seldom dare to utter our names in front of our sisters, but in reality, our community is close-knit, calm, and morally upstanding—those are our habits, including abstinence. We avoid meeting new people; a new face is often a new personality, and we're afraid of introducing dissonance into our harmony. What's more, we're hardly ever sought out, and we're even less interested in others than they are in us.

"Despite our isolation, we keep up with everything that's happening in the world of art," Antoine went on. "Each person takes their turn at gathering news and then brings it back to the group. We read the new books, and when there's a play that's packing in audiences, we arrange for one of us who's interested to go see it. Those are rare pleasures for us, but we keep them alive by remembering them. We're like children who don't often get to play with toys; we make our joys last as long as possible. When the sound has faded, we listen to the echo. One day, will someone and something come forward from our organization? Time will tell. Will we one day produce a great artist? I doubt it. When our muses do appear, we realize they're short of breath. Our products take on the taste of our *terroir;* up till now, they've been sickly. We don't know if we will give birth to great works, but we can produce sincere ones. Despite all the muddle-heads, the loafers, the parasites, the charlatans, and the whole pernicious mob that descends on the arts like a swarm of locusts on a crop, a definitive form of modern art will one day take shape. In the meantime, there are those who are patient, performing useful labor, believing as much as they can despite our era of disbelief, living apart from the uproar surrounding new theories, caring little about childish triumphs, humbly resigned to their modest role. We like to count ourselves among those people. Do you want to join us, now that you know who we actually are?" Antoine looked Francis in the eye.

"I thought you'd never ask!" Francis answered.

"Good!" said Antoine. "I'll arrange for you to meet everyone, but keep thinking about it. You can see from what I've told you, that up till now, being part of our group hasn't always had its benefits."

V. The Initiation

The hour was now late, and the two young men had walked the whole length of the Rue de l'Est at least ten times while they were talking. They finally parted, agreeing to meet again soon.

The next day, Antoine came to visit Francis. "Have you heard the news?" he asked.

"What news?"

"Your paintings have sold."

"And how do you know that?" asked Francis.

"Because I've just come from seeing the person who bought them. I was there when they were delivered. They're now in the parlor of the Russian princess who is taking art lessons from me." Antoine's tone became more brusque: "Speaking of which, you didn't tell me you had arranged with Morin to paint the area above the doorway in the country house of one of his clients."

Francis was astonished to hear this. "We've never even spoken about it."

"But that's what Morin told the princess, and now she wants to speak with you. He even told her that you were already on your way to her country house."

"And why the hell would he have made all that up?" Francis demanded.

"The sale was made two weeks ago," Antoine added. "Morin asked the princess to let him continue showing your paintings for a while."

"Do you know how much she paid for my paintings?"

"A fairly high price," said Antoine, smiling. "But since you're my friend, I did you a nice turn by telling the princess she got a good deal. Morin charged her fifteen hundred francs."

"Oh, now I understand!" exclaimed Francis. "I see why he never told me about the sale and why he was afraid I might meet that lady. He didn't want me to know he'd made such a huge profit on his first sale of my work."

"That's very possible," said Antoine, "and very much in character for Morin. I told the princess that you were still in Paris, and I gave her your address. If that lady wants to give you a commission, which is likely, you can get on a good footing with her and trick Morin by avoiding his enormous cut. The princess spends heedlessly, as you've already seen."

That phrase echoed in Francis' ears, and that little joke about the profits made from his paintings upset him, but he didn't let his resentment show.

"So, you think this lady is going to commission me?" Francis asked.

"Maybe she's going to ask you to create two canvases to match your *Spring* and *Winter.* And now that she knows where to find you, she'll ask for you. And while we're on the subject, the group is inviting you to have dinner with us tonight at our house. We'll toast your joining us. The princess paid me for a month of lessons. Next month won't be as good, because the lady had to cancel her lessons for two weeks. She has relatives visiting from Russia who are going to take up all her time."

"Is she young?" asked Francis.

"Not only is she young, she's pretty, and widowed, and her manners are lovely. She paints more or less like I make tapestries, and she insists that all her friends buy tickets when she raffles off her paintings for charity. I bought a ticket once, and I was polite enough to take one of her paintings home. If there's a grain of vanity in her fantasy of being an artist, the poor are the ones who benefit. Her husband was killed in the Caucasus War, and since she's been free, she's used her freedom like a woman who's known slavery. She has excellent tobacco, and in her house she burns incense from the East."

"Doesn't all that go to your head?" asked Francis.

"Yes, at the beginning, because I wasn't used to the aromas, but I'm starting to get used to them."

"I wasn't referring to the incense," said Francis. "I was asking whether finding yourself in a *tête-à-tête* with a woman you say is attractive, sociable, and unpredictable…What I mean is, do you only talk about painting?"

"We talk about all sorts of things," said Antoine. "Since the princess is opposed to her government, we discuss Polish independence. During her hour-long lesson, I'm the princess' teacher, and afterwards, I seamlessly transition to being her very humble servant. You worry me," added Antoine, laughing. "Are you planning to ask for the princess' hand in marriage? I wouldn't like that, because then you'd take over as her teacher, and our stewpot would once again only be a decoration."

The two young men pressed one another's hands, and then parted, making a plan to meet that evening, when Francis was to be introduced to all of the Water Drinkers.

Morin's conduct toward Francis was weighing heavily on his heart, so Francis went to the gallery to seek an explanation. As soon as their first words were exchanged, Morin cut short the discussion: "I wanted to surprise you, but you found out first. Since I never miss an opportunity to please my artists, I placed an item in a newspaper for tomorrow, 'Madame the Princess of ***, known for her advanced taste in art, has purchased two canvases by Monsieur Francis Bernier, which have lately attracted a crowd to Monsieur Morin's splendid gallery, the meeting place for all the collectors in Paris.' It's short, but it's clear: everyone will get their part, and you'll get a full share, more than we previously agreed. I sold those paintings for much more than I'd hoped, so I decided to give you a bigger piece of the pie. Everyone has to live, my young friend." Morin slipped into Francis' palm a fine and trembling piece of paper, which Francis calmly put in his wallet.

Francis, who was now primed by Antoine to mistrust Morin, suspected that the latter's generosity was a trap. It didn't take long to discover Morin's motive. The dealer then ordered two canvases to match the ones he'd sold. "I'll pay you for them in advance," said Morin.

"On what terms?" asked Francis.

"I don't think you have anything to complain about when it comes to the terms," answered Morin. "I propose a deal to an artist: the artist can take it or leave it. Once the deal is made, it's up to me what arrangement I make with the client. Of course I turn a profit. We don't live in the clouds: we all have our own source of income, and we all try our best to live well by it."

"Then you should not be surprised if I do what everyone else does," said Francis. "For example, going directly to the person who wants to order the two paintings that match the ones she already bought. By making the arrangements myself, naturally I'll benefit from the profit you made from my work. It's just as you said: 'We all have our own source of income, and we all try our best to live well by it.'"

"My dear sir," said Morin, "I was the one who plucked you out of your garret, I showed your work in a good light, and I would like to show it in an even better one. If you think you're already a big enough boy to do without me, do as you please. That'll be a lesson to me not to treat a new artist with such sensitivity."

"In that case," said Francis, "I will have the honor of informing Madame the Princess de *** that I am not in the countryside, as it pleased you to tell her, and that I'm at her service."

"And you are free to do so," said Morin.

Francis went home, and from there to Antoine's, where he was expected. All of the Water Drinkers had assembled there and welcomed him in a way that put him at ease right away. They made a modest meal, but even such a simple dinner gave rise to jokes that showed the guests were not used to eating so well. Francis' initiation involved none of the ridiculous ceremonies he'd heard rumors about.

He was not asked to take any oaths, but the president of the society, a painter named Lazare, took him aside and read to him the rules of the association. Those articles spelled out the same principles Antoine had discussed with him the previous evening. Lazare had Francis read twice the text of Article 5: "The goal of the society being principally to allow each of the members to maintain the strict integrity of his art, no member may diverge from that or create work for commercial purposes, no matter what monetary benefits he might derive from such activity..."

"But how do you know when you're 'diverging' from that integrity?" asked Francis. "Where does art end and a professional career begin? If you have talent, that's proven by your products, and a work of art doesn't lose merit if it's paid for."

"It's not a question of that," said Lazare. "If you have talent, even a lot of talent, you risk compromising it if you spend your time on easy improvisations, or pointless displays of technique, which distract you from real study. Frivolous works take time away from more difficult projects. When you make *fac-similes,* to use the word in its etymological sense of making something similar to another work, you lose the ability to create something true. You start by fooling others, but you end up fooling yourself. That's the explanation for Article 5. If you don't understand it," said Lazare sarcastically, "just raise your hand and I'll be more than happy to repeat it."

"I'll follow that rule and all the others," said Francis, "and I was already partly acquainted with all the clauses of your contract. I came here tonight to accept it."

"So, that's that, then," said Lazare. "The only thing remaining, if this is within your means, is to pay the small amount of dues specified in the last article. These funds, which unfortunately never have time to accumulate, are made available to members for their work expenses. They can't be used for any other purpose, and the material necessities of life, pressing as they may be, are not a reason for anyone to access the account. Those who cannot pay their dues at the specified time are required to settle their arrears as soon as they have the means. Our fund does not loan money. We won't give out even forty sous if you pay twenty minutes past the deadline."

Since it happened to be the first of the month, two members of the society, the only ones who were regularly earning any money, handed their dues over to the President. "Anyone who has a request should speak now," said Lazare, who, it seems, was also the association's treasurer.

"I have a request," said the painter Soleil, who lived in the same apartment as Antoine and Paul.

"Go on," said Lazare.

"Well," said Soleil, looking very embarrassed, "I would like...but you wouldn't approve..."

"Of what?" asked the treasurer, very impatiently. "Go ahead and we'll see."

"Well," Soleil burst out suddenly, as if asking for an enormous favor, "I'd like four francs to buy some cadmium yellow."

"Why not ask for a million francs, while you're at it?" said Lazare. "You're becoming annoying with these conventional colors of yours."

"I can't manage without it for my sunsets," Soleil insisted.

"Then paint the sky after sunset," answered Lazare.

Following this refusal, Soleil made a sad face, half in earnest and half in jest. He claimed that the absence of this very expensive color prevented him from working. "You're just saying bad things about cadmium yellow because you don't know how to use it. You're trying to prevent me from gaining a reputation." And Soleil got up and sat in a corner, looking glum. General laughter accompanied him.

"Just give him his four francs," Antoine said to Lazare. "If he doesn't get them, he'll keep refusing to work."

Lazare relented by loosening the strings of his purse. "Here, take it," he said to Soleil.

"Are you serious?" Soleil's face was beaming with joy.

Francis then told his new associates the story of how he'd broken with the art dealer, and the reason for the split: "You understand that I'd rather deal directly with collectors who are commissioning paintings from me. I'm sure the rules don't forbid me from accepting commissions," he said jokingly.

"Well, actually, that depends," Lazare interjected. "If you're commissioned to create paintings to decorate a grandfather clock, then Article 5 applies. But you're making it sound as if collectors are forming a line on the stairway outside your door."

"Not quite," said Francis, blushing, "but I am hoping to sell two canvaseses to match my *Winter* and *Spring*."

"In fact," said Antoine, "the princess is planning to ask you for those. Speaking of which…" Antoine then showed Francis a pastel in the corner with cracked glass in the frame. "If you'd like to see a portrait of the princess, here it is. She gave it to me the other day to touch up the dress, which is slightly smudged. It's the work of a fellow Frenchman who has set himself up in Russia and doing very well there. If you ask me, I wouldn't even let him clean my palette."

Francis looked at the portrait. "Is it a good likeness?"

"I'd say so. At least the work has that in its favor. So, what do you think?"

"Your student is quite attractive," said Francis. "I have to admit these aristocratic types have something extremely seductive about them."

In the middle of the soirée, the grandmother got home from work. She was not alone. An old soldier accompanied her. "Outside the barracks, I met the quartermaster," she said, "and I brought him here so we could pay his bill."

"Oh, is that you, Father of the 56th?" asked Antoine. "What do we owe you this month?"

"Here's your tab." The soldier took out of his pocket a card like the one used to tally the points in a game of piquet.

"Sixty-six loaves of bread," said Antoine. "That comes to sixteen francs fifty. Did you know, Father of the 56th, that this has been an awful two weeks? We've found all sorts of things in the bread. Everything except flour, in fact."

"The word in the barracks," said the soldier, "is that the brass ain't doin' its duty by the rank and file. But the Minister of War himself took a tour of the commissariat, and he says to them, 'I hereby authorize you not to steal from the government, which is like a father to the foot soldier. I expect to find on my table every day a sample of the military rations, and the first time I bite into a foreign substance, whether it's straw or any other damn thing, I'm gonna drag you and your blasted gaiters in front of a court martial.' Seems to me," continued the soldier in his colorful way, "since then the brass has sent us real bread. Well, it's all the same to me, I sell that bread, anyway. I don't eat none of it. Me, I go to the *boulangerie,* along with the bourgeoisie."

This explanation, which revealed a new detail about the Water Drinkers' life of poverty, darkened Francis' expression. He pulled Antoine aside. "Is that true? Has it come to that?"

"Come to what?" asked Antoine. "Oh, right, the ordinance bread. No worries, ever since the minister got angry about them adulterating the military rations, the bread is perfectly good, and when it's bad, we just eat less of it. That way, we save even more."

"Either way, it's a sad situation," said Francis.

"Well, this isn't Rabelais' utopia, 'The Abbey of Thélème,' where vows of poverty are replaced by the life of an epicure," said Antoine.

"Now I'm one of you, and you told me yesterday, 'Everything that comes in is shared.' So let's share." And Francis showed Antoine the five-hundred franc bill that Morin had just given him.

"You're in too much of a hurry," Antoine insisted, "to apply to yourself a formula that's only a way of expressing our brotherhood for one another. If we were in a bad way, I might accept your offer and thank you for it in the name of all of us. But right now, our little account is in fairly good shape, and besides, you need that money for yourself. It may be a long time before you earn more, now that you've broken with Morin. You need to think of the future and manage your funds well, so you can keep working productively for as long as possible. With that amount of money, you could be your own boss for almost a year, and a year of serious study would be extremely useful to you."

"Make it last a year? Impossible," said Francis.

"Let's say six months, then, since you enjoy your luxuries," said Antoine.

"Bah! I can afford to be a little generous, since I'm about to get a commission that will undoubtedly pay well."

"If I were in your shoes, and I got that commission, I'd ask for some time to finish it," said Antoine.

"But I have nothing else I'm working on."

"You do, actually," said Antoine. "Your work is to make progress."

"You think so?"

"I'm sure of it," continued Antoine. "And while I'm giving you advice about your best interests, I would advise you to find a studio in a different neighborhood. Why don't you move to our neighborhood? It'll be easier to maintain ties between us, and you'll find the rents and the cost of living are lower here. But the biggest advantage for you will be that you won't be subject to the same temptations that you're now faced with all day long, whenever you step outside into that lively and brightly lit neighborhood where you're living. The spectacle of a comfortable life, even when you're not envious of it, makes a life of privation seem sadder. Despite yourself, you feel the influence of your milieu; better that it should be favorable. Living in this area, you'll spare yourself painful comparisons. Seeing people who don't have to work for a living, the tools you use that barely earn your keep feel heavier in your hand."

"I'll think about it," said Francis.

"Do it soon," Antoine concluded.

Since it was getting quite late, Francis shook the hands of all his new friends and said goodnight to them.

"My word!" said Lazare to his friends when their new member had left. "I'm not sure that guy is to really to my liking. From his manners, you get the feeling he bathes in starch every day. We need to rumple him up a bit."

VI. The Russian Princess

Walking home, Francis mulled over his impressions of the evening. Other than Lazare, everyone seemed to welcome him cordially. But he noticed something that might have been self-protective in the words and actions of the other members of the group. He understood why those who were planning to be his friends would speak with a certain frankness, and yet he would have hoped that their free expression would have been a bit more restrained. Two or three times during the evening, they happen to discuss his painting, and the Water Drinkers were extremely generous with their advice, which he didn't doubt was useful, but they were equally stingy with comments that were kind. *Who are they to criticize?* Francis asked himself. *I don't see that they've painted a lot of masterpieces.* And recalling certain parts of the conversation that evening, Francis said to himself, *Despite what they claim, each one of them is hiding a well of bitterness they don't even see, their speech slips into declamations, and there's a kind of affectation in their simplicity. Those who didn't know them and who hadn't seen what they create might well suspect that their disdain for certain art comes from their own inability to create work of that sort. I'm not saying that's the case,* Francis added in his thoughts, as if to protest an opinion that would reflect badly on his new friends, *It's just that one could say that.*

When he arrived back home, the concierge handed him a letter that had been brought that evening by a valet in formal livery. *I know what this is,* Francis told himself while dashing up the stairs four at time. He broke the seal, immediately glanced down to look for the signature, and didn't find one. It was note from the Princess de ***, asking if he had time in his schedule to give her art lessons. She asked him to respond soon, because she was thinking about cancelling with her current instructor. Not one word more. Francis was disappointed; he'd been hoping for a commission for new paintings, and the princess didn't even mention the canvases of his she'd already purchased. This was a blow both to his finances and to his vanity. It wasn't even a letter, it was a just a note written in the most formal language, six lines in an elegant, spidery scrawl that got right to the point, with no signature.

High society and a Tartar to boot! Francis muttered to himself, crumpling the note. *Well, I'm not even going to answer.* He realized that not responding would be very bad manners, so he began seven or eight times to write a response, which he tried to phrase with a dry and dignified impertinence. He finally found a way to refuse her offer that satisfied him, and he promised himself he would send it the very next day. He was so preoccupied with his own feelings that he didn't think for a second that the best reason for refusing to give the princess lessons was Antoine. That thought only occurred to him the following morning. This belated recollection made him rephrase his refusal. He wrote a new letter, this time changing the spiteful tone to one of regret. He didn't explain himself, but he left doubts about the reason behind his refusal. It ended up as a *no* that seemed annoyed not to be able to say *yes*.

Francis thought that it might not be appropriate to just drop a letter of this sort in the mail, so he decided to deliver it in person. Then he remembered he actually had other business in the quarter where the princess lived, so he could leave the letter at her town house. He started to put on his clothes, and imagining it was a beautiful day, he got all dressed up. By the time he walked down to the street, the weather had shifted. Francis engaged a carriage at a nearby stand. Just when he was handing his letter to the concierge at the princess' home, the princess was leaving in her own coach. Francis spotted a woman entering the door of the carriage, recognized the princess from her portrait, and shouted, "This letter is from Monsieur Francis Bernier!"

The princess, who might have heard him, did not stop, and she left the carriage entrance with her retinue. Francis was frustrated, angry at himself. His reproached himself for his hesitation. In the end he gave up, and he did not even deliver the letter.

Back home, he tried to work, but he could not get in the mood. Just as he was about to go out, Antoine arrived, and despite himself, Francis was irritated to see him.

"I came to tell you," said the Water Drinker, "that I've found a studio for you on the Rue Notre Dame des Champs that's twice as big as this one and half as expensive. It has a view of the garden, and you'll be only a ten-minute walk from us. The studio will be vacant in two weeks. I rented it and put down a deposit."

"That was a mistake," said Francis forcefully. "I've never even seen the studio. What if I don't like it?"

Antoine did not take offense at the intensity of Francis' response. "Oh, all studios are more or less the same," he said. "As long as there's good light, it's fine."

"It sounds like there are too many stairs," said Francis.

"What?" answered Antoine, smiling, "I didn't even tell you what floor it's on. It's at street level."

"Then it'll be too damp."

"My friend," said Antoine, "just admit you don't want to be our neighbor."

"I'm not saying that." Francis was becoming more impatient. "It's just that I'm used to my way of life here in this quarter."

"But only yesterday you said you were renouncing several things about your current way of life."

"My dear friend," said Francis, "I'm beginning to find it a little oppressive to belong to a group that prevents its members from living where they like. Besides, there was nothing about that in the rules."

"True, that's missing," Antoine admitted. "But that was an oversight."

"Perhaps. So, what do you think of this" asked Francis, pointing to a sketch he'd done with a composition he was working on.

"Hmm. An allegory of *Autumn.* Does that mean you've already received the commission from the princess?"

"No. The princess wrote to me, but not about a commission. Look at any of those pieces of paper there on the floor. You'll see what her note was about."

Antoine picked up one of the five or six drafts of the letter that Francis had written the previous evening. "Oh! The princess is asking if *you* would give her lessons," Antoine said with emotion. "Well, I was certainly acting as your friend when I gave her your address."

"But you see how I answered her?" asked Francis.

"You haven't sent this to her yet, right? The letter is still here."

"The one you're holding and all those others were just drafts."

"You had to write that many drafts just to tell her no?" Antoine gazed at his colleague with a worried intensity.

"In the end, the princess has my refusal in hand," said Francis. "Rest assured."

Antoine left in a mood less confident than he revealed to Francis. The two young men both felt a crack appear in their newly sealed friendship. Francis didn't visit the Water Drinkers for the next two or three days, and since none of them visited him, this mutual distancing resulted in a cooling off on both sides.

Antoine seems to be giving me the cold shoulder, Francis thought, *when in the end I acted like a loyal friend.*

One evening, Francis received a letter signed by Lazare. It was an official invitation to a special meeting of the entire group.

The day of that assembly, by chance Francis ran into an old friend, and he invited him to dine. As a result, Francis showed up a little late for the meeting of the Water Drinkers.

"We were waiting for you to arrive before beginning," said President Lazare. "We have these official meetings very rarely. The least you could do was to arrive on time."

"I was delayed by a friend," Francis apologized, "and besides, I live fairly far from here."

"All your friends are right here, and they all arrived before you," Lazare continued. "So there's no one who could have delayed you. Concerning the distance from your home, that's actually the topic of tonight's meeting, and why we invited you. Antoine, who serves as recorder of our rules, has read out a new article that he's proposing to add. The article consists of two lines: 'In order to maintain the bonds of camaraderie, which are at the core of our association, it is crucial for the members who comprise it to meet frequently, and those gatherings are more convenient when all of us live within a certain radius of one another. For that reason, every member of the Water Drinkers must live in the same neighborhood as the society's president, who represents the seat of the organization."

"But what if the president moves every three months, for example?" asked Francis.

"Your objection has been anticipated," Lazare responded. "Since I have lodgings that are inexpensive and that I like, I've signed a lease that extends for several years. The motion has been made and will now be put to a vote. All in favor?"

All the Water Drinkers raised their hands except Francis.

"The motion is carried unanimously, with one exception, and immediately becomes part of our rules."

Antoine's brother, who served as secretary, wrote into the rules the article that the association had just approved.

"Given the fact that the implementation of this article could create difficulties," said Lazare, "a delay of three months is granted to members of the society who are in violation of this rule."

The meeting was then adjourned, and Francis left in a huff. Antoine caught up with him.

"What about your commissions?" asked Antoine, walking Francis home.

"I haven't received them," said Francis, "and now I regret it. My dear Antoine, when you see the princess, try to find out her actual intentions about me."

"I'm still waiting for her to ask *me* to return, because she hasn't resumed her lessons," said Antoine.

Two weeks after the meeting, which was one month to the day since the princess had stopped her lessons, Antoine received a note from her. In the note, the princess thanked him warmly, but made it very clear she was ending his role as her instructor. An amount equal to the price of twelve lessons was included with this missive. Since the letter had arrived when Antoine was not at home, the grandmother had subtracted several francs from the total, which she thought was a payment for work already performed.

That day, Antoine had gone out to see Francis, to borrow an engraving from him. When Antoine arrived, Francis had just returned home, and he was dressed quite elegantly. A pair of white gloves was draped over a chair. Before Antoine had said a word of greeting, his nostrils detected the subtle fragrance of rose oil.

"Have you been to Constantinople since I saw you last?" Antoine asked him. And approaching Francis, he realized that this penetrating aroma was emanating from Francis' garments. "Your outfit smells like a commission," added the Water Drinker.

"That's true," Francis confessed. "I've received new ones…"

"Moscovite, by any chance?" Antoine interrupted. "And did the princess happen to mention when she might resume her lessons?"

"Tomorrow," Francis muttered.

It was when Antoine returned home that day that he found the princess' letter with her thanks. He turned completely pale when he was shown the money, and flew into a fury when he discovered that a dozen francs had already been spent from that sum.

"We have to send that money back immediately," said Lazare, who was visiting Antoine's home at the time. "And we have to tell that lady that an artist is not a lackey you hand a month's salary to when you give them the boot. Even though it would be against the rules, if there were still money in the kitty, I'd give to her. But as it happens, we are dead broke."

"Today's November first; Olivier and Léon get paid today. We'll borrow the money from them," suggested Paul.

"Unfortunately," said Lazare, "today is also All Saints' Day. Our friends will only get their wages tomorrow or the day after, and we have to return the one hundred and twenty francs to the princess before tonight."

"What can we sell?" asked Antoine. Just then he saw Soleil warming himself voluptuously, keeping his hands right by the wood-burning stove, which was wafting a gentle heat throughout the studio. "Step away from there," said Antoine, abruptly disturbing his friend's bliss, and he used a pair of pliers to disconnect the wires that attached the stove to the wall.

"What are you doing?" asked Soleil. "It's burning well for the first time since we've used it."

"Help me put out the fire." Antoine was pulling out the half-consumed logs and was then dousing them in a bucket of water that his brother had brought.

"You're putting out the fire!" exclaimed Soleil.

"We can't sell the stove with a fire in it."

"That's true, it would lower the price," said Lazare. Once he understood Antoine's plan, he quickly went out to look for a buyer.

"We're going to sell the wood stove?" Soleil said, wringing his hands.

"If it's alright with you," said Antoine. "And even if it isn't."

Lazare came back, accompanied by a merchant of odds and ends, who bargained for a long time before offering half of what they'd paid for the wood-stove.

Soleil muttered to himself sadly as the merchant took away his find.

Two hours later, the princess received her money back, along with a very dignified note.

That evening, when Francis returned home, he found stuffed into the keyhole of the door of his studio a little piece of paper with a note consisting only of one line: "We have the honor of informing you that your resignation has been accepted. President of the Society of the Water Drinkers."

Incredible! said Francis to himself, philosophically. *But I do wish them the best of luck. As for me, I prefer continuing on a path that I find pleasant to getting stuck in a rut. When it comes to our mutual goals, let's see who ends up getting there first. Their Article 5 about never earning money from your art is ridiculous, and to submit to that is like swimming with a rock tied around your neck.*

So, reader, you might now be wondering whatever became of our Francis Bernier, following his break with the Water Drinkers. Well, Francis became what he was predestined to become: a mediocre artist, a good old chap who had few pretentions as he grew older, realizing that his reputation was a fluke, the result of a trend that he happened to profit from, as even the most honest of men will profit from a mistake that never hurt anyone.

The Funeral Supper

from Scenes of Youth,
[Scènes de la vie de jeunesse],
published 1851

I.

The story I'm about to tell you concerns my late friend, Count Ulric-Stanislas de Rouvres. He was a very good friend; such a good friend, in fact, that I'm expecting him for his funeral supper right now. How can the deceased attend his own funeral supper? Therein lies the tale.

About a year ago, the young Count Ulric de Rouvres suddenly fell into a deep depression and decided to end his life. You might well ask why someone of Ulric's station became so unhappy. He was magnificently positioned in society: young, attractive, rich enough to satisfy his every whim. There was no real reason for him to kill himself. But then again, a reason that provokes you to commit a folly is never reasonable.

In any case, Ulric decided to put an end to his days, and he chose to do the deed in England. Why England? It's the land of spleen. And what, you ask, is spleen? Spleen is a melancholy of the deepest hue, a despair that infects the souls of poets and romantics.

My friend Ulric, once he had been touched by spleen, could not go back on his resolution to put an end to his suffering. So he crossed the English Channel from France, and after a few days in London, he went to stay in a little village in Sussex. There he went back over all his memories; he looked over his former days, the ones of sunlight, and the ones of shadow. Once again he told himself that there was nothing more for him in life, and after putting his affairs in order, he took a pistol and ventured out into the countryside, where he spent a long time looking for the right spot to deliver his soul unto God.

After an hour, Ulric found a place that lived up to all his expectations for the right setting for a suicide. He took his pistol out of his pocket, loaded it decisively, and placed the icy barrel of the gun right against his burning forehead. His finger was on the trigger, poised to squeeze, when he realized he was not alone. Not ten paces away, there was another fellow who was also getting ready to enter the next world.

Ulric walked over to that unfortunate man, whose neck was already in a noose tied around the branch of a tree.

"What do you think you're doing?" demanded Ulric.

"See for yourself," said the other man. From his perfect English, he appeared to be a local. "I'm about to hang myself. Would you lend me a hand? I'm afraid I'm going to botch it if I try doing this alone. I don't have the right equipment."

"How might I be of service to you, sir?" Ulric asked.

"I would be infinitely grateful," answered the other man, "if you would be so kind as to push that log out from under me. I might not have the strength to roll it away when I'm suspended in midair. Might I also ask you not to leave the area until you are certain that the deed has been successfully accomplished?"

Ulric looked with astonishment at this person who could speak so calmly at the moment of his death. He was a man of about twenty-eight or thirty, and his features, outfit, and manner of speaking all indicated that he came from a distinguished family.

"Pardon me," Ulric said, "I am entirely at your disposal and ready to perform the small service you request of me—after all, we must help each other out in this life—but may I know the reason why you wish to die so young? You may confide in me without fearing any indiscretion on my part, since I too, intend to kill myself in the dark of this little woods." Ulric showed the other man his pistol.

"Oh, you want to blow your brains out! An excellent method. It was highly recommended to me. But I prefer the noose. It's so British."

"Are you doing this because of a misfortune you suffered in love?" Ulric asked.

"Oh, no!" said the other. "I'm not in love."

"A financial crisis, then?"

"Not at all. I'm a millionaire."

"Perhaps your ambitions have been thwarted?"

"I'm not at all ambitious."

"Oh, I get it now," said Ulric. "It's because of spleen, ennui..."

"No, I was happy, very content with my life."

"So, what then?"

"Well, sir, since this confidential information seems to be of great interest to you, the reason I choose to die is this: two years ago, at a dinner party, I bet one of my friends that I'd die before he did. The amount we wagered was considerable, and the bet is well known throughout His Majesty's three kingdoms. And since death has not found me since then, if I don't meet it within the hour, I will lose my bet—and I dearly want to win. And there you have it."

Ulric was stupefied.

"Now that you have heard my confession, sir, I will remind you of the promise you just made." And with this, the Englishman stepped up onto the log and tightened the noose around his neck.

"Wait one moment, if you please, sir. I confess I don't have the courage to do what you ask," said Ulric.

"Then why did you interrupt me earlier? I have no time to lose if I'm going to win my bet. It's now ten minutes to midnight, and I absolutely must be dead by twelve o'clock." The Englishman, seeing that Ulric was not going to help him, kicked away the trunk that still connected him to the ground and was suspended in midair.

His death agonies began immediately. Ulric could not bear the sight, and ran to a nearby field.

A half hour later, Ulric returned to the tree, now a gallows, and found the Englishman stiff, immobile, dead as could be. This sight made Ulric reflect. Death appeared to him horribly ugly, and Ulric renounced on the spot his resolution to allow death to lift the suffering that life had placed on his shoulders.

Ulric, however, now found himself in a highly embarrassing situation. Just the day before he had written a letter to one of his friends saying that he was putting an end to his days, and he considered it an act of cowardice to go back on his word. He was afraid of the ridicule that would redound on him when the news got out of his aborted suicide, an event as pathetic in Ulric's eyes as a duel without a resolution.

While hesitating, Ulric chanced to notice a large wallet that the Englishman had left on the ground. Ulric opened it and found quite a few papers, including a newly issued passport in the name of Sir Arthur Sydney. Seeing the deceased's documents, an idea dawned on Ulric. He took his own wallet, which established his identity, and slipped those papers into the deceased man's wallet. Then he placed the Englishman's documents in his own pocket.

Thanks to this ploy, Ulric was able to pass for dead. The announcement of his suicide by the English press was then picked up by French newspapers. Ulric attended his own funeral, and once he had taken part in his own graveside honors in England, he left for Mexico under the name of Arthur Sydney. When he returned to British Isles six weeks later, he wrote to me the story I've just told you.

Because he could still be easily recognized, Ulric chose not to return to the social world. Or should I say, he chose not to mix with that sliver of Paris that those of our class call "the social world."

The news of Ulric's passing elicited much whispering in Paris society, but after a couple of weeks, attention turned to the next scandal. That was a missed opportunity for Ulric, because his attempted suicide might have made quite a hit with the ladies.

II.

I realize I have not provided my gentle readers with much of an explanation of how Ulric de Rouvres came to the decision to commit suicide, a decision aborted under such unusual circumstances.

My friend had made an early entry into society, because he came into his fortune before he reached his majority at twenty-one years of age. Dazzled at first by the dawning of his twentieth year, and stunned for a moment by the din of the social world he was called upon to inhabit—Ulric hesitated. Like a traveler who, on setting foot for the first time in an unknown land is afraid of getting lost, he sought out a guide.

Guides presented themselves to him by the dozen. Just as with cities that offer many curiosities, at the gates of society a crowd of cicerones loudly offered their services to him.

Ulric, intoxicated by his freedom, wished to hold and behold everything. Ardent, curious, impatient, he wanted to drink all of life's pleasures in a single gulp.

Rapidly he lived, and rapidly he learned. By the age of twenty-four, he had already earned an advanced degree in being a man.

His mind full of bitter knowledge, his youth turned to ashes, and his soul still full of insatiable desires, he left society, which, four years earlier, he had entered with a twinkle in his eye and his chin up. Damaged and filled with sadness, he swelled the ranks of those who pour over all things their suspicions and their brash negativity.

At this point I was the only one of Ulric's friends still in contact with him. One day he came to visit me, and what he said left me no doubt about what he was contemplating.

"Twenty-four seems young to enter the next life," I said to him. "In any case, I hope you won't mind if I don't follow you there. So it's true what they say about you, that you've caught the *mal du siècle,* the illness of our time. You've read Goethe's *Faust* too many times, and the melancholy spirits who followed him. More than anything else, you've been brought to the edge by the influence of people of that sort. You think you're dead, but you're just numb, my dear friend! When you run too much, you're exhausted. That's natural. You're in a period of repose, but tomorrow or the next day you'll toss your morbid resolution out the window along with those English pistols of yours, and you'll give them to some poor devil of a misunderstood poet, whose only cure for the miseries of this world is to enter the next one."

"I was just like you," I continued. "Many times I put the key in the door that leads to the unknown. But I turned back, and I hope you will, too. You'll tell me you have neither the heart nor the soul for it, and it's impossible for you to believe in anything. First of all, we always have our hearts, and as long as they keep ticking, we don't need to ask anything more from them. And as for the soul, a million volumes have been written about it in every language, trying to explain it, without our knowing any more about its existence or its meaning. Soul rhymes with goal; that's about all we know so far."

But my mockery was quite familiar to Ulric, who was already a poet of materialism and an apostle of skepticism. Instead of calming him, my words only spurred him on. I changed my tune and used a language that was more persuasive and paternal. At least for the moment, I succeeded in getting him to renounce his thoughts of suicide.

From that day on, however, Ulric no longer came to visit me. Despite all my efforts, I lost touch with him and did not know what had become of him.

Ulric disappeared from sight for six months. One day I went riding in the countryside near Paris with a few friends. By chance, I ran into Ulric. He was not alone that day; on his arm was a young woman eighteen or twenty years old, dressed like a common worker, and Ulric was similarly clothed. Ulric, whose attire had previously been the last word in elegance; Ulric, who had been the barometer of taste in clothing, whose fashion innovations, no matter how audacious, were always copied by everyone else; if one day Ulric was seized with the idea of putting on red gloves, the next day the entire Jockey Club was wearing them. When I ran into Ulric on my ride outside Paris, he was unrecognizable, dressed in rags from some Herculaneum ruin. And yet I did recognize him at first glance, and when I rode over to speak with him, he shook his head to indicate I should not acknowledge him. Of course, I wondered what mystery could be afoot, but I only found out much later.

In the naïve tales of storytellers and poets of the Middle Ages, there are many adventures of melancholy princes and knights who escape courts and castles to explore the back roads, concealing their high birth and fortune. Disguised as a penniless troubadour, the nobleman wanders, guitar in hand, crooning of love, searching for that one woman who will love him for himself. He trades a sigh for a smile, and pauses under the humble window of a female vassal as readily as he would visit a chatelaine's balcony, emblazoned with its noble coat of arms.

A child of this century, Ulric de Rouvres' ancestors were probably among those heroes, half-poets, half-paladins, who people those old legends. He seemed to want to reintroduce the tradition of those backward days into the civilized customs of our times. And that is exactly what Ulric did to break completely with a social world where for four years his extremely delicate nature was constantly getting bruised.

After converting his entire fortune to an annuity, Ulric entrusted the funds to an attorney engaged to invest them as he saw fit. Ulric had all his possessions auctioned off: the furnishings of his home, which were the epitome of luxury and modern elegance; his retinue; and his horses, some of which were thoroughbreds with an aristocratic pedigree. The proceeds were consigned to the attorney in charge of his fortune. Ulric kept only two hundred francs for himself.

Anyone who came to visit Ulric at his former lodgings on the busy and fashionable Chaussée-d'Antin was told that he no longer resided there. He left no forwarding address.

Using the nondescript name Marc Gilbert, Ulric found a place to live on one of the darkest streets in the Saint-Marceau neighborhood. His dwelling was a sort of working class barracks where from morning to night you could hear the ruckus of three hundred different trades.

Accustomed to the exquisite comforts of the milieu where he had always lived, Ulric went with no transition from extreme opulence to extreme destitution. His room was one of those dark and damp hovels where the sun doesn't dare to send a single beam, afraid it would be held prisoner in that airless dungeon. The furniture was the sort that belonged to the poorest artisan.

That was where Ulric took refuge, where he tried to immerse himself in a new life. Seeing his neighbors, the workers, leave in the morning for their jobs with a song on their lips, and seeing them return from their labors in the evening, doubled over from exhaustion, their faces drenched in sweat but still with the look of peaceful contentment that goes with having completed a task, Ulric said to himself, *These are the real people, the honest people, who knead with their own hardworking hands the bread they eat in the evening.*

It's in them, or nowhere, that I'll find humanity at its best. It's here, or nowhere, that I can cure that invincible sadness that followed me to this garret, where I still find that gnome named Disgust perched at the foot of my bed.

He made a plan, and he began immediately to carry it out. A week later, Ulric, still using the name Marc Gilbert and now clothed in the typical worker's blue smock, managed to get taken on as an apprentice in one of the larger manufacturing businesses in the neighborhood. After six months, he had mastered his trade well enough to be hired as a worker. He chose on purpose one of the most exhausting jobs, one that required more strength than intelligence. He made himself into a living machine, a tool of flesh and bones. And seeing his fingers gloriously mutilated by the holy scars of labor, he hardly recognized himself in the robust form of Marc Gilbert, he, the elegant Ulric de Rouvres, whose hand could have fit, without ripping it, into the glove of the Princess Borghese.

Meanwhile, despite the rough work Ulric daily devoted himself to, in the midst of the workplace, loud as it was, the clamor that surrounded him could not drown out the chorus of despairing voices that continued to echo in his thoughts.

When he returned to his room after a day of hard work, Ulric could not even enjoy the deep sleep that wafts onto the straw pallets of the workers. Insomnia kept watch by his bedside, and no matter what he did to banish it, his thoughts fell into an abyss that every night grew deeper, and which he always emerged from more bitter and less hopeful.

Ulric's heart had that fatal leprosy known as the love of kindness and goodness, and the hatred of evil and injustice. But a strange destiny, which dogged his footsteps, seemed always to deny his instincts and mock the poetry of his hopes. Everything he touched left his hands with a residue of filth, everything he'd known engraved contempt or disgust into his soul, and like soldiers who can count the battles they've fought by their wounds, each of his loves was counted by a betrayal.

Ulric thought, *It is justice that those who are welcomed in life with the golden smile of privilege should be disinherited of happiness, the one thing that can't be bought or inherited. The destiny of the privileged is announced to them at birth: You will live among the powerful, in the half of the world that the other half envies. You will have wealth and rank. As a child, all your whims will be law. As a youth, every pleasure will parade past you, and all your fantasies will blossom. As an adult, every road will be open to your ambition. You will be one of the world's fortunate ones. But your happiness will only be an illusion, and each of your joys will have its shadow, because you will live in a society where corruption is almost a necessity of life, and betrayal is a weapon you need to have always close at hand, like a soldier with his sword.*

Not only that, those born in the most unfortunate circumstances, with no other protection than their own hands, yoked to one type of work, in the hard life that their fate presses on them, they have to keep intact the good instincts they're endowed with. Honesty, gratitude, all the most noble human qualities must sprout in the furrows watered by the sweat of their work. Because of the harshness of their life, the workers must practice brotherhood. Owning nothing, the worker is not acquainted with the hatreds that spring from competing interests. The sympathies and friendships of a worker are spontaneous and sincere, and unlike those in high society, they last longer than a pair of gloves or a corsage. Their loves are not tainted alloys, as in the fashionable world, where love is based on ambition, pride, and sometimes even hate, but is never real love.

Such were Ulric's thoughts.

When he started his employment in the workshop, Ulric's lack of muscles, the distinguished pallor of his complexion, and the whiteness of his hands, which until then had remained idle, earned him irony and insults. At first resigned to the humble role of an apprentice, Ulric endured without complaint all the gibes he was subjected to because of his physical weakness and his manner of speaking, which had nothing in common with the vocabulary in workingmen's taverns. Later on, when he had built up his strength by practicing his trade, when the wear and tear of work had calloused his hands and had colored his complexion with a more virile skin-tone, those who had harassed him quickly changed the way they spoke and acted toward him, when they saw that his once frail arms now lifted the heaviest burdens as easily as a storm lifts a feather off the ground.

As I mentioned, after six months of laboring in the workshop, Ulric knew his tasks well enough to pass his apprenticeship and become a worker. After a year, Ulric, whose intelligence did not escape the attention of his bosses, was made a foreman. This promotion caused a concert of jealous grumblings among his coworkers. On the day when Ulric arrived at his job to take on his new role, the complaints reached such a level that the bosses had to intervene.

"What's going on here?" demanded the owner of the workshop, stepping into the middle of the workers who were in revolt.

"What's going on? We don't want 'Monsieur' here as our foreman," said one of the workers, pointing to Ulric.

"And why the hell not?" asked the owner.

"Because it's humiliating that he's ordering us around now. Just six months ago, he was still an apprentice."

"So, what does that prove?" asked the owner.

"It proves," continued the worker, "that we're all equal, and that this is unjust. There are guys who've worked here ten years, and they're furious that some stranger walks in here and just like that, he gets the first promotion that comes up."

"Yeah, right, it's unjust!" the other workers chimed in.

"Down with Marc Gilbert!" someone yelled, and the others began to chant: "Down with *Monsieur*! Down with *Monsieur*!"

"And not only that," continued the worker who had spoken first, "how come you fired Pierre as the foreman? Pierre was a good guy. And he was supporting a wife and kids."

"Silence!" yelled the boss. "Not another word out of you. I don't have to answer to you, I do as I please. If Pierre did something that made him lose his job, he's doubly guilty since he should have thought about his wife and his children. Pierre was lazy and he encouraged everyone else to be lazy. You think he was a good guy because he counted the hours you spent in the tavern as work. To me, Pierre was a thief."

The workers began to gripe about this, but the owner stopped them with one gesture. "I said *thief,* and I meant *thief.* Anyone who gets paid without earning it, is dishonest. Pierre abused my trust. I gave him some slack, because I knew he was the breadwinner of a family, but the more I indulged him, the more he took advantage of me. I was guilty of not treating my business partners fairly by keeping on someone who was not serving their interests. Honesty depends on duty; I did mine, which was to send Pierre packing. It was even more my duty to hire a replacement who is honest, hardworking, and intelligent. Is it my fault that among the workers who've been here ten years I couldn't find one who was qualified for that job? Is it my fault that the apprentice everyone was bossing around six months ago turned out to be the only one of you worthy of being the supervisor here? You were talking about equality just now. Well, it just so happens that you're not the equal of Marc Gilbert. Those who preach equality to you are crazy. You yourselves know that the men who work the hardest and the best should be paid more than the others. So that's why, starting today, Marc Gilbert is your foreman. Respect and obey him the way you'd do with me. And if you don't like it—that's the door, right over there."

The workers then returned to work without saying a word.

That man is just, Ulric thought, admiring the owner.

"Monsieur Marc Gilbert," said the owner, calling him over for a private conversation. "You started here a year ago as an apprentice. I've made you my second-in-command today, not as a favor to you, but because you earned it. I hope you're happy, and that a year from now you'll get promoted again. But since you're young and you don't have all the experience this job requires, you're going to start at a salary that's two-thirds of what your predecessor earned. It's still a nice piece of change, though."

Ulric was stupefied by these contradictory words.

Some justice! he muttered to himself. *You replace a lazy worker who lacks intelligence and moral probity with a man who has both those qualities plus dedication, and without taking into account the benefits that his management and loyalty will bring to the organization, you pay the honest man less than the thief!*

In one week's time, Ulric's new responsibilities and authority won him a crowd of sycophants. Those who'd been the hardest on him and the least indulgent in the past were the ones who now fawned over him the most, precisely the ones who had spoken against his promotion. He now had real-life experience of the "noble qualities" that sprouted in the furrows watered by the sweat of labor. His heart was soon filled with a new disgust, seeing men who should have been linked in solidarity, spying on each other and denouncing one another's peccadillos, hoping that Ulric would reward them by forgiving their own.

And so, in the lower classes of society, in the world of workers' blue smocks, Ulric found the same corruption, the same dishonesty, the same violent oppression of the weak by the strong. There as elsewhere, every vice was king in the realm of selfishness. All noble instincts were nailed to the cross of self-interest. There, too, every virtue had its Judas and its Pilate. There, too, even more than elsewhere, Ulric had proof that ingratitude, which of all human traits has the least need for cultivation, sprouted right from our inner core.

In the ranks of high society, in the world of white ties and black suits, Ulric had encountered the entire hideous family of human vices. At least there, however, those vices were elegantly dressed, spoke with beautiful diction and correct grammar, and never undertook the slightest action without proper decorum. Often at a salon, Ulric had shaken with pleasure the right hand of a man who was betraying him with his left hand, but that hand was impeccably gloved. Often Ulric believed the smiles of treacherous women. He let himself be moved by the emotional solos they performed in public after much rehearsing, as a performer does with a piano sonata or an opera aria. Ulric was duped, but at least the women who fooled him were bedecked in silk and velvet. Pearls and diamonds, which were torn from nature's mysterious jewelry boxes, used their flare and sparkle to compete with the women's glances, the gems resplendent on their foreheads like a constellation of terrestrial stars. Those women were the queens of the world; they bore names already enshrined in history, and when they walked across a ballroom, they left a wake of perfumes and graces, while the men formed a path of genuflecting admirers.

Ah, Brotherhood! Ulric groaned *It's an elusive phantom, a word that resounds like an alarm bell to inspire revolt. It's easy enough to inscribe that word on banners and on the pediments of monuments. But future centuries added to past centuries are hardly enough to engrave it on the hearts of men.*

Heated Romance in a Cold Spell

from Sketches of the City and the Theater
[Propos de ville et propos de théâtre],
published 1853

During the harsh winter of 1852–53, the extreme cold in Paris forces the cancellation of the usual high society fancy-dress balls, parties, and other social gatherings. Murger describes how this actually benefited heated affairs.

There are two types of people affected by this sudden and unexpected arrival of winter: *husbands,* and *lovers.*

Husbands rubbed their hands together, not just to keep warm, but out of satisfaction. Thanks to the scarcity of balls and soirées, these *messieurs* were able to save many of their usual expenses. For them, making it from one end of a Paris winter to the other was more dangerous than it was for a capitalist to cross a Spanish sierra. Ordinarily, December, January, and February are like bandits, but instead of daggers and blunderbusses held to your throat, those months menace you with bills. It's useless to resist the necessary expenditures. But this cold wave warmed the hearts of husbands. The tabs from jewelers, designers, and dressmakers seemed incredibly moderate. Expenses for 1853 started out at half the amount of previous years. Husbands quickly transferred this surplus in the column for household expenses to the sum that the gentlemen set aside for their "boys' nights out," when the money ran through their fingers and into the hands of the ladies of the demimonde.

But all these plans were brutally thrown to the winds!

Paris social life in the second half of February turned out to be as wild as a youth who has just come of age, and March promises to be no less extravagant. Because the husbands counted on not spending much money this winter, they now have to pay double. Bills for *Madame,* brought up the grand staircase, and bills for *Mademoiselle,* delivered by the back stairs, all pluck a sizable amount from *Monsieur's* wallet in the morning.

As for the lovers, "their suffering was no less cruel," to use the parlance of romance novels. The same situation that initially gladdened the hearts of husbands also added to the security of lovers. Soirées were rare, and balls practically nonexistent. The adored one sat by her fire, relaxing in her cozy armchair, while during the day her husband went to work at the Bourse, the stock exchange. Evenings, after supper, the husband ran to his club, or pretended he was called away to a business meeting. Ah, the inexhaustible mine of excuses!

For this reason, the woman's lover was lord and master, not just of his lady's heart, but of her home. He could keep track of all her visitors: the unwelcome ones, the strange ones, the jealous, and all those rival gentlemen who were to the lover what the husband was to him. The lover might as well have brought over his bathrobe and slippers! He had all the benefits of a domestic life without the expense. The lover had no rivals, and since he didn't have to defend himself, he didn't have to fight. There were no obstacles to his enjoyment. He was confident of being desired and waited for. And he arrived as regularly and as punctually as midnight follows eleven o'clock. The lover's usual chair reached out its arms to welcome him. The fire greeted his arrival with a burst of flames and a bouquet of sparks. The houseplants wafted their most subtle perfumes to him. The curtains slid open and their silk folds deepened. The lamp softened its bright light and filled the boudoir with a discreet semi-darkness, perfect for intimate secrets. By the fireside, the lovers built castles of happiness on the sands of the word *forever.* They gossiped a little about those not present, but not the husband. Nary a quarrel, nor an annoyance. It was charming, delicious.

At midnight, the lover slipped out and the husband returned. The next day it started all over again.

Lovely, no? But too good to last.

Now the social events are starting up again with a vengeance. Today, a ball at the home of the Marquise de ***, tomorrow at the townhouse of Madame ***, the day after, here, and the day after that, yet another. Time to bid adieu to untroubled security, and to the almost endless *tête-à-têtes*!

The mistress wakes up as a woman, and the woman becomes a Parisian again. She puts on the corset she wears to fancy dress balls and won't take it off for two months. Every night she will waltz, mazurka, and redowa around the clock. And the lover, if he wants to keep his conquest, has to be seen at those dances, choked by his white ascot. Wherever his mistress goes, he has to follow her like a shadow, a melancholy and sorry shadow, casting wary glances at his desired one, like a miser who sees his safe opened and its riches displayed to men who overtly covet them.

Every soirée is a battlefield, every ball a combat of one against a hundred, because in order not to lose an inch of ground in his mistress' heart, he has to be as witty as all the other men who court her put together; his cravat has to be tied as elegantly, the line of his leg must be perfect now that culottes are back in fashion for men and have added a new means of seduction; a well-turned calf, according to our ancestors, was considered irresistible in their time.

The first stroke of the violin's bow, when Paris takes its place for the first contradance, which lasts until the first green leaves unfold, has already ended many affairs. The pair hardly see one another, or rather they only see one another under the bright lights of chandeliers, when they happen to bump into one another. All around him, the lover hears remarks that are as disturbing to his vanity as they are unsettling to his heart. Speaking about his mistress, a nosy friend says to him, "Since you know Madame So-and-So, do you think it's true that Armand has taken the place of Paul on her private dance card?" It's so amusing to hear that, if your name is neither Armand nor Paul!

Or it might be her husband, whose witticisms are snowballing with the passions that his wife is inspiring, who pulls the lover aside and says to his prey with a smirk, "Take a look, old chap—do you see how beautiful my wife is this evening! What shoulders! I'd never really noticed them before."

During the daytime, Madame sleeps, to recover from the exhausting nights. If she receives at all, it's only for an hour or two. If the lover is admitted, it's only in the company of her other suitors, and his mistress flirtatiously gives them all an audience, reserving for the others her most tender words and manners. That way she will have a veritable Roman legion greeting her when she makes her next entrance at a ball. If she deigns to allow the lover a quarter of an hour for a *tête-à-tête,* he wastes it with jealous quarrels: "Why did you dance two numbers in a row with Monsieur So-and-so?" "Why did you wear a blue dress when you know I abhor that color?"

The poor woman wanted a lover, and all she gets now is a judge at her trial. True, the two of them do patch things up, and they both take advantage of that reconciliation, but it doesn't matter. After enough of these little spats, love starts to resemble an old plate with ten cracks glued together. One fine day it will break beyond repair, and nothing can be done with the pieces.

So, at the end of this season of social gatherings, balls, and soirées, how many couples will be uncoupled, how many intimate alliances drawn up on pink paper and delivered in person with a lover's oath will be torn up by dallying, how many pretty mouths that say one name today will whisper a new one tomorrow?

Translator's Acknowledgments

The translator sends his deepest thanks those who read the manuscript of this book and made crucial contributions to the text: Renée Morel, always the most eagle-eyed and knowledgeable reader and critic of translation drafts; Itaï Kovacs and Jerrold Siegel, scholars and experts on Henry Murger and the Water Drinkers, for their encouragement; and Esta Brand, who made great suggestions on how to adapt the text to make it tastier. The drawing of the artist on page 13 is a portrait of one of the real-life Water Drinkers. The image is used by permission of the Bibliothèque de l'Institut national d'histoire de l'art (INHA), Jacques Doucet collections, MS 515, Piece 23. Gratitude to the editors of the *Chicago Quarterly Review*, for publishing "The Funeral Supper" in their journal.

ZACK ROGOW (translation and adaptation) was the co-winner of the PEN/Book-of-the-Month Club Translation Award for *Earthlight* by André Breton (Black Widow Press), and he also translated Breton's *Arcanum 17* (Green Integer). Rogow won the Bay Area Book Reviewers Award for his translation of George Sand's novel, *Horace* (Mercury House). His English version of Colette's novel *Green Wheat* (Sarabande Books) was shortlisted for the PEN/Book-of-the-Month Club Translation Award and for the Northern California Book Award in Translation. Rogow's co-translation of *Shipwrecked on a Traffic Island and Other Previously Untranslated Gems* by Colette was published by State University of New York Press. He edited two volumes of *Two Lines: World Writing in Translation.* www.zackrogow.com

BLACK WIDOW PRESS :: POETRY IN TRANSLATION

Approximate Man and Other Writings by Tristan Tzara. Translated and edited by Mary Ann Caws.

Art Poétique by Guillevic. Translated by Maureen Smith.

Beginnings of the Prose Poem. Edited by Mary Ann Caws, Michel Delville.

The Big Game by Benjamin Péret. Translated with an introduction by Marilyn Kallet.

Boris Vian Invents Boris Vian: A Boris Vian Reader. Edited and translated by Julia Older.

Capital of Pain by Paul Eluard. Translated by Mary Ann Caws, Patricia Terry, and Nancy Kline.

Chanson Dada: Selected Poems by Tristan Tzara. Translated with an introduction and essay by Lee Harwood.

Earthlight (Clair de Terre) by André Breton. Translated by Bill Zavatsky and Zack Rogow. (New and revised ed.)

Essential Poems and Prose of Jules Laforgue. Translated and edited by Patricia Terry.

Essential Poems and Writings of Joyce Mansour: A Bilingual Anthology. Translated with an introduction by Serge Gavronsky.

Essential Poems and Writings of Robert Desnos: A Bilingual Anthology. Edited with an introduction and essay by Mary Ann Caws.

EyeSeas (Les Ziaux) by Raymond Queneau. Translated with an introduction by Daniela Hurezanu and Stephen Kessler.

Fables in a Modern Key by Pierre Coran. Translated by Norman R. Shapiro. Full-color illustrations by Olga Pastuchiv.

Fables of Town & Country by Pierre Coran. Translated by Norman R. Shapiro. Full-color illustrations by Olga Pastuchiv.

A Flea the Size of Paris: The Old French Fatrasies & Fatras. Edited & translated by Ted Byrne and Donato Mancini.

Forbidden Pleasures: New Selected Poems 1924–1949 by Luis Cernuda. Translated by Stephen Kessler.

Furor and Mystery & Other Writings by René Char. Translated by Mary Ann Caws and Nancy Kline.

The Gentle Genius of Cécile Périn: Selected Poems (1906–1956). Edited and translated by Norman R. Shapiro.

The Great Madness by Avigdor Hameiri. Translated and edited by Peter C. Appelbaum; introduction by Dan Hecht.

Guarding the Air: Selected Poems of Gunnar Harding. Translated and edited by Roger Greenwald.

Howls & Growls: French Poems to Bark By. Translated by Norman R. Shapiro; illustrated by Olga K. Pastuchiv.

I Have Invented Nothing: Selected Poems by Jean-Pierre Rosnay. Translated by J. Kates.

In Praise of Sleep: Selected Poems of Lucian Blaga. Translated with an introduction by Andrei Codrescu.

The Inventor of Love & Other Writings by Gherasim Luca. Translated by Julian & Laura Semilian. Introduction by Andrei Codrescu. Essay by Petre Răileanu.

Jules Supervielle: Selected Prose and Poetry. Translated by Nancy Kline & Patricia Terry.

La Fontaine's Bawdy by Jean de La Fontaine. Translated with an introduction by Norman R. Shapiro.

Last Love Poems of Paul Eluard. Translated with an introduction by Marilyn Kallet.

A Life of Poems, Poems of a Life by Anna de Noailles. Edited and translated by Norman R. Shapiro. Introduction by Catherine Perry.

Love, Poetry (L'amour la poésie) by Paul Eluard. Translated with an essay by Stuart Kendall.

Of Human Carnage—Odessa 1918–1920 by Avigdor Hameiri. Translated and edited by Peter C. Appelbaum with an introduction by Dan Hecht.

Pierre Reverdy: Poems, Early to Late. Translated by Mary Ann Caws and Patricia Terry.

Poems of André Breton: A Bilingual Anthology. Translated with essays by Jean-Pierre Cauvin and Mary Ann Caws.

Poems of A.O. Barnabooth by Valery Larbaud. Translated by Ron Padgett and Bill Zavatsky.

Poems of Consummation by Vicente Aleixandre. Translated by Stephen Kessler.

Préversities: A Jacques Prévert Sampler. Translated and edited by Norman R. Shapiro.

RhymAmusings (AmuseRimes) by Pierre Coran. Translated by Norman R. Shapiro.

The Sea and Other Poems by Guillevic. Translated by Patricia Terry. Introduction by Monique Chefdor.

Sixty Years: Selected Poems 1957–2017 by Mikhail Yeryomin. Translated by J. Kates.

Through Naked Branches by Tarjei Vesaas. Translated, edited, and introduced by Roger Greenwald.

To Speak, to Tell You? Poems by Sabine Sicaud. Translated by Norman R. Shapiro. Introduction & notes by Odile Ayral-Clause.

The Water Drinkers and Other Sketches of Paris in the Romantic Era by Henry Murger. Translated & adapted by Zack Rogow.

BLACK WIDOW PRESS :: MODERN POETRY SERIES

RALPH ADAMO
All the Good Hiding Places: Poems

WILLIS BARNSTONE
ABC of Translation
African Bestiary (Forthcoming)

DAVE BRINKS
The Caveat Onus
The Secret Brain: Selected Poems 1995–2012

RUXANDRA CESEREANU
California (on the Someș). Translated with Adam J. Sorkin.
Crusader-Woman. Translated by Adam J. Sorkin; Introduction by Andrei Codrescu.
Forgiven Submarine, with Andrei Codrescu.

ANDREI CODRESCU
A Possible Epic of Care, with Vincent Katz
Forgiven Submarine, with Ruxandra Cesereanu
How to Live Under Fascism (Forthcoming)
Too Late for Nightmares: Poems

CLAYTON ESHLEMAN
An Alchemist with One Eye on Fire
Anticline
Archaic Design
Clayton Eshleman/The Essential Poetry: 1960–2015
Grindstone of Rapport: A Clayton Eshleman Reader
Penetralia
Pollen Aria
The Price of Experience
Endure: Poems by Bei Dao. Translated with Lucas Klein.
Curdled Skulls: Poems of Bernard Bador. Translated with Bernard Bador.

ROGER GREENWALD
An Opening in the Vertical World
Keener Sounds. A Suite.

PIERRE JORIS
Barzakh (Poems 2000–2012)
Exile Is My Trade: A Habib Tengour Reader

MARILYN KALLET
Even When We Sleep
How Our Bodies Learned
Packing Light: New and Selected Poems
The Love That Moves Me
Disenchanted City (La ville désenchantée) by Chantal Bizzini. Translated by J. Bradford Anderson, Darren Jackson, and Marilyn Kallet.

ROBERT KELLY
Fire Exit
The Hexagon

STEPHEN KESSLER
Garage Elegies
Last Call

BILL LAVENDER
Memory Wing

HELLER LEVINSON
Crossfall (Forthcoming)
from stone this running
jus' sayn'
LinguaQuake
Lure
Lurk
Query Caboodle
Seep
Shift Gristle
Tenebraed
Un-
Valvular Ash
Wrack Lariat

JOHN OLSON
Backscatter: New and Selected Poems
Dada Budapest
Larynx Galaxy
Weave of the Dream King

NIYI OSUNDARE
City Without People: The Katrina Poems
Green: Sighs of Our Ailing Planet: Poems

MEBANE ROBERTSON
An American Unconscious
Signal from Draco: New and Selected Poems

JEROME ROTHENBERG
Concealments and Caprichos
Eye of Witness: A Jerome Rothenberg Reader. Edited with commentaries by Heriberto Yepez & Jerome Rothenberg.
The President of Desolation & Other Poems

AMINA SAÏD
The Present Tense of the World: Poems 2000–2009. Translated with an introduction by Marilyn Hacker.

JULIAN SEMILIAN
Osiris with a trombone across the seam of insubstance

ANIS SHIVANI
Soraya (Sonnets)

JERRY W. WARD, JR.
Fractal Song

ANTHOLOGIES / BIOGRAPHIES

Barbaric Vast & Wild: A Gathering of Outside and Subterranean Poetry (Poems for the Millennium, vol. 5). Edited by Jerome Rothenberg and John Bloomberg-Rissman.

Clayton Eshleman: The Whole Art by Stuart Kendall

Revolution of the Mind: The Life of André Breton by Mark Polizzotti

Henry Murger (1822–1861) was one of the leading writers of the Romantic movement. His most famous book is Scenes of Bohemian Life, *the source of Puccini's* La Bohème *and Jonathan Larson's musical* Rent. *A man-about-town in Paris, Murger died a tragic death at age thirty-eight, hastened by a disease called purpura, which turns the skin a purplish hue. A statue of Murger stands to this day in the Jardin du Luxembourg in Paris. His writings have not reached many English-language readers up till now because so few of his works were translated.*